UNDER THE HARROW

Center Point
Large Print

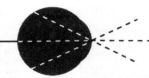

**This Large Print Book carries the
Seal of Approval of N.A.V.H.**

UNDER THE HARROW

Flynn Berry

CENTER POINT LARGE PRINT
THORNDIKE, MAINE

This Center Point Large Print edition is published
in the year 2016 by arrangement with Penguin Books,
an imprint of Penguin Publishing Group,
a division of Penguin Random House LLC.

The text of this Large Print edition is unabridged.
In other aspects, this book may vary
from the original edition.
Printed in the United States of America
on permanent paper.
Set in 16-point Times New Roman type.

ISBN: 978-1-68324-131-7

Library of Congress Cataloging-in-Publication Data

Large Print
Fiction

Names: Berry, Flynn, 1986– author.
Title: Under the harrow / Flynn Berry.
Description: Center Point Large Print edition. | Thorndike, Maine :
Center Point Large Print, 2016.
Identifiers: LCCN 2016028057 | ISBN 9781683241317
   (hardcover : alk. paper)
Subjects: LCSH: Sisters—Fiction. | Murder—Fiction. | Large type
books. | Psychological fiction. | GSAFD: Suspense fiction.
Classification: LCC PS3602.E76367 U53 2016b | DDC 813/.6—dc23
LC record available at https://lccn.loc.gov/2016028057

To J. A. B.

Come, what do we gain by evasions?
We are under the harrow and can't escape.
—C. S. Lewis, *A Grief Observed*

➤ Contents ✦

PART ONE

HUNTERS

→ 1 ←

A woman is missing in the East Riding. She vanished from Hedon, near where we grew up. When Rachel learns of the disappearance, she will think it's him.

The hanging sign for the Surprise, a painting of a clipper ship on a green sea, creaks in the wind. The pub stands on a quiet road in Chelsea. After finishing the job on Phene Street, I came for lunch and a glass of white wine. I work as an assistant to a landscaper. Her specialty is in meadows. They look like they haven't been landscaped at all.

On-screen, a reporter moves through the park where the woman was last seen. Police and dogs fan out across the hills behind the town. I could tell Rachel about her tonight, though it would ruin our visit. It might not have anything to do with what happened to her. The woman might not have even come to harm.

The builders at the house across the road have finished eating, the white paper bags balled at their feet, and are leaning back against the steps in the cold sunshine. I should have already left for the train to Oxford, but I wait at the bar in my coat and scarf while a detective from the station in Hull asks the public for any information about the disappearance.

When the broadcast moves to the storm in the north, I leave under the hanging sign and turn on the next corner toward Royal Hospital Road. I walk past the trimmed squares of Burton Court. Past the estate agent's. Sunny homes in Chelsea and Kensington. I still live in a tower block in Kilburn. The stairwell forever smelling of fresh paint, seagulls diving at the balconies. I don't have a garden, obviously. The cobbler's children have no shoes, etc.

Black cabs drive down Sloane Street. Blurry orbs of light glow on the sides of buildings, reflected from the facing windows. The book-shop displays a pile of new translations of *The Thousand and One Nights*.

In one of the stories, a magician drank a potion made from an herb that kept him young. The problem was that the herb grew only at the top of a mountain, and so every year the magician tricked a youth into climbing the mountain. Throw down the herb, said the magician. Then I'll come get you. The youth threw down the herb. I can't remember the end. That may have been it. I've forgotten the ending for most of the stories, except the important one, that Scheherazade lives.

A few minutes on the tube, and then I am back out again, hiking up the stairs to Paddington station. I buy my ticket and a bottle of red wine at the Whistlestop.

On the platform, the train engines hum. I wish

Rachel would move to London. "But then you wouldn't get to come here," she says, and I do love her house, an old farmhouse on a shallow hill, with two ancient elms on either side of it. The sound of the elms soughing in the wind fills the upstairs bedrooms. And she likes living there, living alone. Two years ago she almost got married. "Close brush," she said.

On the train, I press my head against the seat and watch the winter fields pass by the window. My carriage is empty except for a few commuters who have left work early for the weekend. The sky is gray with a ribbon of purple at the horizon. It's colder here, outside the city. You can see it on the faces of people waiting at the local stations. A thin stream of air whistles through a crack at the bottom of the pane. The train is a lighted capsule traveling through the charcoal landscape.

Two boys in hoods run alongside my carriage. Before I draw level with them, they jump a low wall and disappear down the berm. The train plunges through a tight hedge. In summer, it turns the light in the carriage green and flickering, like being underwater. Now, the hedge is bare enough that the light doesn't change at all. I can see small birds in the gaps of the branches, framed by vines.

A few weeks ago Rachel mentioned that she plans to raise goats. She said the hawthorn tree at the bottom of her garden is perfect for them to climb on. She already has a dog, a large German shepherd. "How will Fenno feel about the goats?" I asked.

"Demented with happiness, probably," she said.

I wonder if all goats climb trees, or only certain types. I didn't believe her until she showed me pictures of a goat balanced at the edge of a fan of cedar, a group of them in a white mulberry. None of the pictures showed how the goats climbed the tree, though. "They use their hooves, Nora," said Rachel, which doesn't make any sense.

A woman comes down the aisle with a trolley and I buy a Twix bar for myself and an Aero for Rachel. Our father called us greedy little girls. "Too right," said Rachel.

I watch the fields trundle by. Tonight I'll tell her about my artist's residency, to start two months from now in the middle of January. Twelve weeks in France, with lodging and a tiny bursary. I applied with a play that I wrote at university called *The Robber Bridegroom*. It's embarrassing that I haven't done anything better since then, but that no longer matters because in France I will write something new. Rachel will be pleased for me. She will pour us a celebratory drink. Later, over dinner, she will tell me stories from her week at work, and I won't tell her about the missing woman in Yorkshire.

The train sounds its horn, a long, low call, as it passes through the chalk hills. I try to remember what Rachel said she would cook tonight. I see her moving around in her kitchen, shifting the massive slate bowl of chestnuts to the edge of the counter. Coq au vin and polenta, I think.

She likes to cook, partly because of her job. She says her patients talk all the time about food, now that they can't eat what they want. They often ask what she makes, and she likes to give them a good answer.

Clay roofs and chimney pots rise above a high brick wall alongside me, and then it wraps around, enclosing the village. Past the wall is a field of dry shrubs and hedges with a few paths tunneling through it. At its edge, a man in a green hat tends a trash fire. Charred leaves rise on the drafts and spin into the white sky, floating over the field.

From my bag, I take out the folder of properties to let in Cornwall. Over the summer, Rachel and I rented a house in Polperro. Both of us have time off at Christmas and plan to book a house this weekend.

Polperro is built into the folds of a coastal ravine. Whitewashed houses with slate roofs nestle in the green rivulets. Between the two cliffs is a harbor and, past a seawall, an inner harbor, large enough for maybe a dozen small sailing boats, with houses and pubs built to the water's edge on the quay. When the tide is out, the boats in the inner harbor rest on their hulls in the mud. On the western hook of the ravine are two square merchant's houses—one a tweed-brown brick, the other white. Above them, umbrella pines stand outlined against the sky. Past the merchant's houses, on the point, a fisherman's croft is built into the rocks. The croft is made of rough granite, so on foggy days it blurs into the stones around it. The house we rented was on a headland ten minutes' walk along the coast path from Polperro and included a private staircase with seventy-one steps built up the cliff from the beach.

I loved Cornwall with a mad, jealous ardor. I was twenty-nine and had only just discovered it, but it belonged to me. The list of things I loved about Cornwall was long but not complete.

It included our house, of course, and the town, the Lizard Peninsula, and the legend of King Arthur, whose seat was a few miles up the coast at Tintagel. The town of Mousehole, pronounced "mouzall." Daphne du Maurier and *Last night I dreamt I went to Manderley again,* and of course you did, anyone who left here would. The widow's walks. The photographs in pubs of wrecks, and of townspeople in long brown skirts and jackets, dwarfed by the ruined hulls.

Every day the list had to be rewritten. I added the umbrella pines and the Crumplehorn Inn. Cornish pasties and Cornish ale. Swimming, both in open water and in the quiet, dripping caves. Every minute, really, even the ones when we were asleep.

"Everything's better here," I said.

And Rachel said, "Well."

"What's your favorite thing about Cornwall?" I asked, and she groaned. "Or I can tell you mine."

But then she said, "Well, to start, there's the ocean."

If anything, she loved it more than I did, and she is even more excited than I am to go back. She hasn't been herself lately. She seems frayed by her work, and always tired.

At the next station, the conductor warns the riders of possible delays tomorrow from the storm. Excellent, I think, so it is going to snow.

We pass through another town, where the cars now have their headlights switched on, pale yellow marbles in the weak afternoon light, and then the train curves around a poplar hedge and straightens as it pulls into Marlow.

Rachel isn't at the station. This isn't unusual. Her shifts at the hospital often run late. I leave the platform under a light so dull that the roofs of the town already seem to be dusted with snow. I walk away from the village toward her house, and soon I am on the open stretch of the road, a narrow tarmac ribbon between farms.

I wonder if she is walking to meet me with Fenno. The bottle of red wine thumps against my back. I picture Rachel's kitchen. The bowl of chestnuts, the polenta bubbling on the hob. A car drives toward me, and I step onto the verge. It slows to a crawl as it approaches, and the woman behind the wheel nods at me before accelerating down the road.

I walk faster, my breath warming my chest, my cold fingers curled in my pockets. Heavy clouds mass overhead, and in the quiet the air takes on a tinnitus ring.

And then her house is in sight. I climb the hill, and the gravel crunches under my feet. Her car is parked in the drive, she must have just gotten home. I open her door.

I stumble back before I know what is wrong with the house, like something has flown at me.

The first thing I see is the dog. The dog is hanging by his lead from the top of the stairs. The rope creaks as the dog slowly rotates. I know this is bad, but it is also amazing. How did you do that, I wonder.

His lead is wrapped around a post on the banister. He must have tangled it and fallen, strangling himself. But there is blood on the floor and the walls.

I am hyperventilating, though everything around me is calm and still. It is urgent that I do something, but I don't know what. I don't call for Rachel.

I climb the stairs. There is a stripe of blood on the wall just below my shoulder, like someone sagged against it while climbing. When the stripe ends, there are red handprints on the step above it, and the next step, and then on the landing.

In the upstairs hallway, the stains turn messy. I

don't see any handprints. It looks as though someone crawled or was dragged. I stare at the stains and then, after some time, I look down the hall.

I can hear myself keening as I crawl toward her. The front of her shirt is black and wet, and I gently lift her onto my lap. I put my hand to her neck, trying to feel her pulse, then lower my ear to her face to hear her breathing. My cheek brushes her nose and chills sweep down my neck. I blow air into her mouth and pump on her chest, then stop. It might cause more damage.

I bend my forehead to Rachel's and the hallway goes dark. My breath rolls on her skin and into her hair. The hall closes around us.

My phone never has service in her house. I'll have to go outside to call an ambulance. I can't leave her, but then I am stumbling down the stairs and through the door.

As soon as the call ends, I can't remember what I said. There is no one in either direction, just her neighbors' houses and the ridge behind them, and in the humming quiet I think I can hear the sea. The sky roils above me. I look up. Put my hands to my head. My ears ring as if someone is shouting very loudly.

I wait for Rachel to appear in the doorway. Her face confused and exhausted, her eyes fixing on mine. I am listening for the soft pad of her footsteps when I hear the sirens.

She has to come downstairs before the ambulance arrives. It will be finished when someone else sees her. I beg her to come down. The sirens grow louder, and my ears lift away from my jaw like I am grinning. I watch the door for her.

And then the ambulance is in view, racing down the road between the farms. It comes up her drive, gravel spraying from its tires, and when the doors open and the paramedics run to me, I can't speak. The first paramedic enters the house and the second asks if I am wounded. I look down, and my shirt is stained with blood. When I don't answer, he begins to examine me.

I pull away from him and run up the stairs behind the first paramedic. Rachel's face is turned to the ceiling, her dark hair pooling on the floor, her arms at her sides. I can see her feet, in thick woolen socks. I want to crawl around the woman and squeeze them between my hands.

The paramedic points at a place on Rachel's neck, then touches the same place on herself, under her jaw. I can't hear her over the sounds I am making. She helps me down the steps. She opens the ambulance doors and settles me on its ledge and puts a foil wrapper around my shoulders. The wet on my shirt turns cold and plasters the fabric to my stomach. My teeth chatter. The paramedic switches on a fan so heat pours from the ambulance behind me, warming my back, escaping in vapors into the cold air.

Soon patrol cars arrive, the police in black uniforms gathering on the road and coming up the lawn. I stare at them, my eyes streaking from one face to the next. Static crackles from someone's belt. I wait for one of them to smile and give the game away. A constable lowers a stake into the dirt and runs tape across the door, the ribbon bobbing up and down as it unspools behind him.

The edges of my vision go soft, then disappear entirely. I am so tired. I try to watch the police so I can tell Rachel what this was like.

The sky foams, like the spindrift of a huge unseen wave is bearing down on us. Who did this to you, I wonder, but that isn't the important thing, the important thing is that you come back. At the house across the road, the open barn where they usually park is empty. An Oxford professor lives there. "The gentleman farmer," Rachel calls him. Beyond the professor's house, the ridge is an almost vertical cliff face, with steep paths cut into the stone. I stare at the ridge until it seems to come loose and start to drift closer.

No one goes into the house. They are all waiting for someone. The constable who ran the tape stands in front, guarding the entrance. In the paddock next door to the professor's house, a woman rides a horse. Her cottage stands behind the paddock, near the foot of the ridge. The horse and rider gallop in a great circle under the darkening sky.

As the woman leans forward into the wind, I

wonder if she can see us. The house, the ambulance, the uniformed police standing on the lawn.

A door slams at the bottom of the driveway and a man and woman step onto the gravel. Everyone watches the pair advance up the hill. They both wear tan coats, their hands in their pockets, their coattails blowing behind them. Their gaze is trained on the house, then the woman looks in my direction and our eyes catch. I am buffeted by wind, cold air. The woman lifts the tape and enters the house. I close my eyes. I hear footsteps approaching on the gravel. The man kneels down next to me. He waits.

Color sweeps over my eyelids. It will settle soon to black, and then I will hear the elm trees soughing overhead. If I go down the stairs, I'll see our dishes in the sink and on the hob. The scrapings of polenta dried to the bottom of the pot. The chestnut skins on the counter, dropped where we pulled them off, burning our fingers.

If I go to her room, I'll see the shadows of the southern-planted elm flickering on the boards. The dog asleep, sprawled below the bed, near enough that Rachel can drop her arm over the edge of the mattress and pet him. And Rachel, asleep.

I open my eyes.

→ 2 ←

The man kneeling next to me says hello. He is holding his tie against his stomach. Behind him, the wind flattens the grass on the hill.

"Hello, Nora," he says, and I wonder if we have met before. I don't remember telling anyone my name. He must know Rachel. He has a large, square face and hooded eyes, and I try to place him at an event in town, bonfire night or the fire brigade fund-raiser. "DI Moretti. I'm from the station in Abingdon."

It is a blow. He has never met her, her town doesn't have murder detectives. To file any serious complaint you probably have to go to Oxford or Abingdon. As we walk down the drive, two women in white forensic suits pass us on their way to the house.

As we drive away I can't breathe. I look out the window at the line of plane trees flashing past. I would have thought it would feel like a dream but it doesn't. The man driving next to me is real, the landscape outside the window is real, and the wet sticking my shirt to my stomach, and the thoughts coiling through my head.

I want the shock to buy me a little more time, but the grief is already here, it came down like a guillotine when the woman put her finger to

Rachel's neck. I keep thinking how I am never going to see my sister again, how I was about to see her. As we drive through Marlow, I realize that I am talking to myself in my head. No one else is there. Usually when I have the uncanny sensation of watching myself think, I shape my thoughts into things to tell Rachel.

I shrink against the seat. Cars rush past us on the motorway. I wonder if the detective is always such a slow driver, or only when he has someone else in the car. I realize I haven't been watching the road signs to check where he is taking me. Part of me hopes he will take me to a dark, wet field, far from the lights of the town. It would be symmetrical. One sister murdered and then the other, in the space of a few hours.

He did it. Then circled around the house and came up the drive, and convinced me to leave with him while everyone else was distracted. It isn't hard to persuade myself. The fear is already here, pressing under the surface. I take a pen from my bag and grip it under my thigh.

I wait for him to ease onto one of the turnings, for an abandoned factory, or an empty orchard. Dead space surrounds the motorway, he has a lot of options. I ready myself to stab the pen into his eye, and then run back to her house. Rachel will be sitting in her living room. She will look up, frowning. "Did it work?"

But the sign for Abingdon appears, and the

detective turns off the motorway, slowing to a stop at the end of the slip road. His face is slack, his eyes trained up through the windscreen at the signal.

"Who did it?" I ask.

He doesn't look at me. The indicator ticks in the quiet car. "We don't know yet."

The signal changes and he pulls the car into gear. The light box sign of the Thames Valley Police revolves on a post at the entrance to the building.

In an open-plan room upstairs, a fair man with a dark suit hanging from his shoulders stands in front of a whiteboard. When he hears us enter, he shifts away from the board, where he has just taped up a picture of Rachel.

I groan. It is the picture from the hospital website, her oval face framed by dark hair. Her face is so familiar it is like looking at myself. She is paler and has stronger bones in her face. I can disappear in a room, she can't. Both of us have high cheekbones, but hers turn out like knobs. She smiles in the photograph with her mouth closed, her lips pressed a little to the side.

In the interview room, Moretti sits down across from me, unhooking the button of his suit jacket with one hand.

"Are you tired?" he asks.

"Yes."

"It's the shock."

I nod. It's strange to be so tired, and also so scared, as if my body is asleep but receiving electric jolts.

"Can I get you anything?" he asks. I don't know what he means, and when I don't answer he brings me a tea that I don't drink. He hands me a navy sweatshirt and tracksuit bottoms. "If you'd like to change."

"No, thank you."

He talks for a few minutes about nothing. He has a cabin at Whitstable. It is beautiful, he says, at low tide. He makes me nervous, even while talking about the sea.

He asks me to tell him what I saw when I first entered the house. I can hear my tongue lift from the bottom of my mouth with a click before every answer. He rubs at the back of his neck, the weight of his hand pushing his head down.

"Do you live with her?"

"No, I live in London."

"Is it common for you to be there on a Friday afternoon?"

"Yes. I often come up to visit."

"When was the last time you spoke to your sister?"

"Last night, around ten."

The sky has darkened, so I can see the pale citrine squares of office lights across the road.

"And how did she sound?"

"Like herself."

Above his shoulder, one of the yellow tiles clicks off. I wonder if he thinks I did it. It doesn't seem likely, though, and my fear of it is distant, another depth charge but one that barely reaches me. For a moment, I wish I were being framed. Then, what I felt now would be something else—worry, outrage, righteousness—other than this. Which is nothing, like waking in a field with no memory of how you got there.

"How long will this last?" I ask.

"What?"

"The shock."

"It depends. Maybe a few days."

In an office across the street, a cleaning woman lifts the cord of a vacuum and shifts chairs out of her path.

"I'm sorry," he says. "I know you must want to go home. Have you noticed anything weighing on Rachel recently?"

"No. Her work, a little."

"Is there anyone you can think of who might want to harm Rachel?"

"No."

"If she felt threatened, would she tell you?"

"Yes."

None of this is like her. I can just as easily see the other outcome. I can see Rachel, drenched in blood, sitting in this chair and patiently explaining to the inspector how she killed the man who attacked her.

"Did it take a long time?" I ask.

"I don't know," he says, and I bow my head against the ringing. The woman who came up the drive with him opens the door. She has a soft, pouchy face and curling hair pulled back into a knot. "Alistair," she says. "A word."

When he returns, Moretti says, "Did Rachel have a boyfriend?"

"No."

He asks me to write down the names of the men she dated in the last year or so. I print each letter neatly, starting with the most recent and going back sixteen years, to her first boyfriend in Snaith, where we grew up. When I finish the list, I sit with my hands curled on the table in front of me, and Moretti stands near the door with his heavy square head bent to the paper. I watch to see if he recognizes any of the names from other cases, but his expression doesn't change.

"The first name," I say. "Stephen Bailey. They almost got married two years ago. She still saw him sometimes. He lives in West Bay, Dorset."

"Was he ever violent toward her?"

"No."

Moretti nods. Stephen will still be the first person to eliminate. The detective leaves the room, and when he returns his hands are empty. I think of the pub this afternoon, and the missing woman in Yorkshire.

"There's something else," I say. "Rachel was attacked when she was seventeen."

"Attacked?"

"Yes. The charge would have been grievous bodily harm."

"Did she know the assailant?"

"No."

"Was anyone arrested?"

"No. The police didn't believe her." They would allow that she had been assaulted, but not in the way she described. They suspected that she had tried to rob or solicit someone and been violently rebuffed. They were the last of the old wave of policemen, preoccupied with the amount she'd had to drink, and that she didn't cry. "It was in Snaith, Yorkshire. I don't know if they still have a record of it. It was fifteen years ago."

Moretti thanks me. "We need you to stay in the area. Do you have anywhere to sleep tonight?" he asks.

"Rachel's house."

"You can't stay there. Is there someone who can come pick you up?"

I am so tired. I don't want to try to explain this to anybody, or to wait in the station for one of my friends to arrive from London. When the interview ends, a constable drives me to the only inn in Marlow.

I hope we crash. A lorry holding metal poles drives in front of us on the Abingdon Road, and I

29

imagine the nylon ribbon snapping, the metal poles falling out, dancing on the road, one of them pinioning me to the seat.

The Marlow high street is curved like a sickle, with the common at one end and the train station at the other. The Hunters is at the bottom of the sickle, next to the train station. It is a square, cream stone building with black shutters. When the constable drops me at the inn, there are a few people waiting on the train platform, and they all turn to look at the police car.

At the Hunters, I lock the door and put on the chain. I run my hand along the papered wall, then press my ear to it and hold my breath. I want to hear a woman's voice. A mother talking to her daughter, maybe, as they get ready for bed. No sounds come through the wall. Everyone's probably sleeping, I tell myself.

I turn off the lights and crawl under the blanket. I know what's happening is real, but I do keep expecting her to call.

⇒ 3 ⇐

We are supposed to drive to Broadwell today for lingonberry crêpes and the museum, I think when I wake, angry that our plans have been postponed.

Halfway between the bed and the bathroom, my knees crumple. I collapse, but it's like being yanked upright. The dog rotates from the ceiling. Rachel lies curled against the wall. There are red handprints on the stairs. There are three clean posts on the banister and a dirty one with the dog's lead tied around it.

I don't know how long I stayed like that. At some point I decide to wash myself. I can't shower, because I think I can smell her house in my hair. Instead I strip and run a damp flannel over my body, watching its fabric turn pink and brown.

I dress, put my clothes from yesterday into a plastic bag, and carry them to the skip behind the inn. This feels strange, like I am disposing of evidence, but the police didn't ask me to keep them. They should have advised me more carefully. I walk past a painting of a fox hunt in the hall, with some of the red riders hidden behind the trees.

As I climb the stairs, Moretti calls to say he has a few more questions for me. "I'm doing a press statement in an hour. My statement won't include anything about the dog."

"Why not?"

"People fixate on that sort of thing. I can't prepare you," he says, "for what it will be like if this becomes a national story. We can't tell you not to talk to the press, but I can say it won't help the case. They will get in the way, and then when they get bored they will look for what makes Rachel interesting."

"What makes her interesting?"

"The worst things about her."

A constable will collect me from the Hunters at five. I decide to wait in my room. I have six hours on my own until he arrives, and I wonder if I will make it until then.

A few hours later, there is a knock at the door. "I've had some complaints from the other guests," says the manager of the inn. Behind her, the lamps are switched on in the hall. She wears a scarf of Black Watch tartan, and I want to tell her that I used to live in Scotland. My sister came to visit me there.

"The noise is disturbing them."

"I'm sorry." I have to lean on the door frame. I haven't had anything to eat or drink today. Food is going to be a problem.

"Let me know if there's anything you need," she says. "I'm so sorry. It's been such a difficult time. First Callum and now your sister."

"Callum?"

"The young man from town, killed in an accident on the Bristol Road. He was only twenty-seven."

I remember now. Rachel was one of his nurses. I consider sharing with the woman what Rachel told me about him, but decide against it.

At five, a constable collects me and we drive to Abingdon. In the interview room, Moretti says,

"We haven't been able to find your father. Are you in touch with him?"

"No."

"Was Rachel in touch with him?"

"No."

The heating pipes click in the ceiling above us. Outside the night is heavy with clouds. It is already snowing in Lancashire and Cumbria. The detective hasn't asked about our mother. He must already know that she died a long time ago, soon after I was born.

"When did you last speak to your father?"

"Three years ago."

"Does he have a history of violence?"

"No," I say, though I'm not sure that's entirely true. "He's also frail. Rachel was much stronger than him. Do you have to tell him about her?"

"Yes."

They will have a hard time finding him. He stopped collecting benefits after becoming suspicious of the government. Rachel had a postcard from him a few months ago saying he was in Blackpool, which I decide not to tell the detective.

"Have you spoken to Stephen yet?" I ask.

"He was at his restaurant all day."

The news comes as a relief, and I feel disloyal for suspecting him. He adored her.

Moretti says, "What type of vehicle does your father drive?"

"He doesn't drive anymore," I say, and start to explain. He's an alcoholic, though the word has always sounded too polished to describe him. Moretti must already know some of this. He has a record. Disorderly behavior, trespassing, burglary.

A constable knocks on the door, and Moretti excuses himself. I look into the incident room. One of the detectives is eating chips from a packet of foil and paper, and the air smells of vinegar.

I wish Fenno were with me, sitting on his haunches beside my chair. I want to rest my hand on his soft head. I gave him a bath on my last visit, cupping my hand over his eyes while rinsing the soap from his fur. When I wrapped him in a towel he leaned against me, and we stayed like that for a long time, the warm damp soaking through my shirt.

When Moretti returns, he says, "What we need from you now is an account of anything unusual in Rachel's routine. It could be as small as a change in her route to work. Any new friends, a new activity."

"I don't know. She talked about joining a gym in Oxford so she could swim in the winter, but she hadn't yet."

"Anything else? Any changes at the hospital?"

"No."

"Did she enjoy her work?"

"Yes, mostly." She had a difficult time early in

her career, when she was studying to become a nurse practitioner while already working as a registered nurse. She told me that she would bicycle home hoping someone would hit her so she could lie down. "She said it was demanding, but it satisfied her."

Moretti studies me, and I wonder if I am trying his patience. Soon our interview will end, and I will have to leave. I can't imagine what I will do next.

"Do you want something to drink?" he asks, and I nod. While he fixes us tea, I try to think of something to tell him, but I can't remember any changes in her habits. I read the brochure from Victim Support. "Life can fall apart after a murder," it says. "Simple things like paying bills and answering the phone can become difficult."

I want to ask Moretti what he does in Whitstable, and how often he goes there. I expect to tell Rachel about all of this, and it is something she will want to know. We drink our tea in silence.

"On Sunday Rachel said she was off to meet someone named Martin."

Moretti turns to me. "And where did they go?"

"She didn't say. It was the evening, so dinner somewhere, I think. I asked if it was a date and she said no. She said he was a friend from the hospital."

"His surname?"

"She didn't tell me."

Moretti says, "When did Rachel decide to move?"

"She wasn't moving."

"She visited an estate agent two weeks ago."

"Where was she going?"

"St. Ives." The north coast of Cornwall. I have a pulse of excitement. I love St. Ives. I'll get to visit her there. "Rachel planned to move, and she didn't sleep at her house this week. We think it's likely she was being threatened."

"Where was she staying?"

"With Helen Thompson."

Moretti stands and I follow him from the room, too baffled to protest. He says, "Sergeant Lewis is on his way to Marlow. He's offered to drop you at the hotel."

A tall black man with a South London accent meets me in the corridor. In the lift on the way down, he says, "I'm sorry about your sister."

When the doors open, I follow him outside to his car. Rain begins to drum the windscreen as we work our way through the traffic.

"Where do people go afterward?" I ask.

"They go home," he says. The wipers sluice water from the glass.

"How long have you been a policeman?"

"Eight years," he says, leaning forward at a crossing to check the oncoming traffic. "I give myself two more."

⇒ 4 ⇐

Rachel bought her house in Marlow five years ago. Her town is perfect. There are painted-wood buildings on the high street. There is the common. There are the yews on the long end of the common. There is the yellow clock in the village hall. There are the two pubs. There is the church and the church graveyard. There is the rill. There is the petrol station.

The Duck and Cover is the tradesmen's pub. It used to be called something different, the Duck and Clover, until someone painted out one of the letters. The Miller's Arms is the commuters' pub. It serves Pimm's and shows sports only during the World Cup and Wimbledon. Rachel thought there was going to be an explosive showdown between the two sides eventually. She hoped for one. She sided firmly with the Duck and Cover. She said, "We don't want it to turn into Chipping Norton." She said, "It's important that the people who work here can afford to live here."

With the exception of the Miller's Arms, the town hasn't changed much, or not yet. There are no clothing or housewares shops on the high street. The village has a spring fête, and a pasta dinner to raise money for the firehouse.

"Why weren't there as many commuters before?" I asked her.

"The trains got faster."

There is another, larger town with the same name near London, with a famous pub, but Rachel never corrected people when they confused the two, or when they told her they had been to the Hand and Flowers.

Rachel said there was something wrong with the town. I can't remember exactly when this happened. It was recent, sometime after we got back from Cornwall. I didn't let her finish. We were eating breakfast at her house. I had just woken up, and I didn't want to hear it. I knew from her tone of voice that what she was about to tell me was horrible. I knew I had to stop her. I had a raspberry croissant and an espresso and I had her town.

There is the wine shop. There is the building society. There is the gold rooster on top of the Hunters. There is the library. There are the twins who work for the town. There is the yellow awning of the Miller's Arms. There are the poplars in front of the repair garage.

I thought the twins were one person until I saw them both at once washing a bin lorry. They both wore mirrored sunglasses and they both kept their hair long and they both had rottweilers.

"Do they have identical dogs?" I asked.

"No, there's just one dog," said Rachel.

• • •

The Hunters isn't doing very well. There are twelve rooms and only two other guests. It's November, but according to Rachel no one stayed there in the summer either. She said it only stayed open because of the bar below the rooms. This is good news for me, since I am not planning to leave.

When I return from the police station, I steal a carving knife from the kitchen. I put it under my bed, so if I drop my arm over the edge I can reach it. Then I sink down on the bed, wondering what she wanted to tell me, and let the darkness swarm my face.

⇒ 5 ⇐

The first passengers are already waiting in the darkness on the train platform when I go out to buy the papers at the newsagent's shop across the road the next morning and carry them back to the empty front room at the inn. The room has green wallpaper with gold lilies of the valley. It's where the riders used to eat breakfast before a hunt.

Rachel isn't in the *Telegraph*. She isn't in the *Independent*, the *Sun*, the *Guardian*, or the *Daily Mail*. If none of the national papers reported it, maybe it didn't happen.

But she is on the cover of the *Oxford Mail*.

The reporter must have had a copy of the postmortem. She died from arterial bleeding, I learn. The time of death was between three and four in the afternoon. She was stabbed eleven times in the stomach, chest, and neck. She had defensive wounds on her hands and arms.

I am at the table reading the article and then I am on all fours on the carpet. The pattern in the wallpaper starts to move. My mouth gapes.

When the worst of the pain recedes, I am washed against the corner of the room. I put the newspapers in the empty fireplace. I want to burn them, but I don't have any matches.

I call the landscaper. I tell her there has been a death in the family and that I don't know when I will come back to London. The phrasing pleases me, like it wasn't Rachel who died, but someone else in the family, an aunt, our dad. She tells me to take all the time I need, but she doesn't offer paid bereavement leave. I don't really blame her. It isn't that sort of job.

I call my best friend, Martha. She wants to come stay with me but I say I need to be alone at the moment.

"When are you coming home?" she asks.

"I don't know. The detective asked me to stay in the area."

"Why?"

"They need information about her, I think."

I ask Martha to tell our other friends, and I give

her the numbers for Rachel's as well. Alice lives in Guatemala. I don't have her number, and I hope Martha can't find it either. It comforts me that to her Rachel is alive and well, like that makes it partially true.

After the calls, I walk to her house. It is a Sunday afternoon in late November, and a few people drive past me, going about their errands. I can't believe that I plan to survive her, to go on into life without her. The road to her house, a stripe of black tarmac, stretches in front of me.

The newspaper article didn't mention the dog. The police must be pleased. I still see him, hanging from the top of the stairs. A large German shepherd. I'm surprised the banister post could hold his weight.

In the early dusk, uniformed figures move in the long grass at the edge of Rachel's lawn. I leave the road in front of her neighbor's property and walk around the horse paddock. Behind it, a path climbs the ridge.

I walk slowly, stopping sometimes to use my hand for balance on the rocks, until I am across the valley from Rachel's house. All the lights are on, and figures move in the upstairs windows. I count eighteen people searching in the grass, under the roiling sky. The blue tape is still stretched across the door and a man in uniform stands beside it.

Snow starts to fall. A gust of white smoke billows up over the cliff edge. Someone is in the professor's house below the ridge. I lean over until I can see its roof and chimneys. Twists of steam rise, melting into the snow. The professor is walking up the drive, throwing handfuls of yellow sand and salt. At the edge of his property he looks across the road to Rachel's house. His shoulders slump, and the empty paper bag hangs at his side.

He stands there, waiting, I think, for someone to come down the hill so he can ask if there is any news. They will have interviewed him already. I imagine there are tears in his eyes. He liked Rachel. And I think he must have been scared last night, maybe unable to sleep.

I look up, my chest raw and aching. The snow stops, hovers, swirls in fast horizontal gyres. I walk toward the spine of the ridge, away from the cliff edge, through a band of low, twisting trees. They are barely taller than my head, stunted by the wind. A branch jabs out from one with a piece of stiff yellow fabric hanging over it. I step onto a flat rock, and when I come down its other side, I land in a mess of beer cans and cigarette ends. The back of my neck prickles and heat rushes over my skin. I look up slowly and there, framed in a gap between the trees, is Rachel's house.

The branches form a portrait oval around it. In the dusk I can see people moving through the rooms of her house. As night falls, the pictures in the windows will grow sharper and clearer. She didn't have any curtains, except for one in the bathroom. I can see its white gauze, but even that reaches only to the sash. You would be able to see the top of her head when she stood at the sink to brush her teeth, when she came out of the shower.

Someone drank Tennent's Light Ale and smoked Dunhills and watched her. I search the ridge behind me. I pick up a sharp rock and turn in a circle, so the litter and dry leaves crackle under my boots. I wait for a man to appear. I'm not frightened, I want to see who did this to her. As the minutes pass, the chance that someone else is here sags, then collapses.

Through the gap in the branches, I watch the snow fall on her house. The ridge is so quiet I think I can hear the snow as it lands on the frozen ground. An absolute bleakness takes hold of me. The men searching the grounds move deeper into the woods. I notice the snow melting on the cigarette ends, so they soften and expand.

I call Lewis, whose car is parked at the bottom of her lawn. I watch him duck under the tape and come out of the house. He stands on the drive in a dark overcoat. In the silence, I watch him take the phone from his pocket and check the screen.

"Hello, Nora."

"I found something."

"Where are you?"

I scramble out onto the path, in front of the thorn trees, and start to wave. "Here."

He rotates his head, then sees me. He stops. His face is a distant blur, his tie twisting in the wind, his trousers bagging above his shoes.

By the time I hear him on the path, I am frozen. As he steps into the gap in the trees, I know from his expression that I look absurd.

Lewis stares at me, his face slackened and sad, through the portrait oval of the branches. Two more years, he said in the car, but I can see he wishes it were none. The thorn branches arch above him.

He ducks under them and kneels to look at the ground. I wonder if he expects to find nothing, that I have been guarding nothing. As he stands, he turns and sees the house, framed by the gap in the trees, in a perfect oval, as though someone cut back the branches. His shoulders drop.

"Someone was watching her," I say.

"Nora," says Lewis, "why did you come here?" He stands a head taller than me, and he addresses the question into the space above me.

"I wanted to see the house."

He nods, staring over the cliff. "Did you think someone was watching Rachel?"

"No."

We look at the valley, and the stands of trees forming dark pools in the white snow. In daylight, a man would be invisible up here, and at night

44

he could move closer. I imagine him circling the house, putting his hands on the windows.

A man in a forensic suit—the thin fabric stretched over his shoes and pulled taut over his head—comes up the path. Lewis asks him to bag the material, and we start down the ridge. Ahead of me Lewis leaves a trail of footprints on the snow. Off the far side of the ridge, the forest below is a series of crosshatches.

We scramble down the rock and emerge behind the paddock. I follow Lewis to the road, my legs growing heavy as we trudge through the snow.

"Are you hungry?" he asks.

The Emerald Gate has plastic tables and photographs of the dishes backlit above the till. A young man in chef's whites lifts a metal basket from a fryer and shakes it before letting it submerge again, and the smell of oil makes my mouth water. My last full meal was two days ago, at the pub in London.

I watch the pearls of jasmine open in my tea, groggy and fascinated. My fists push my cheeks up to my eyes. Lewis slides his knees under the table, looking too large for his chair. I rub my thumb over my cheek, which was scratched by the thorn trees.

Our food arrives on the counter. Lewis ordered moo shu pancakes, and I'm having the same, since I couldn't face making a decision. The rhythm of it calms me, spooning the mixture onto a thin flour pancake, folding it into a triangle, dipping it into the plum sauce. We assemble and eat in silence as the snow drifts under the street-lamps.

"Nora," he says, "why did you go to the ridge?"

"I told you, I wanted to see the house."

Behind the counter, the cook ladles wonton soup into a plastic container, and the salty smell of the broth drifts over to us.

"Did Rachel ever say anything to make you think to look there?"

"No." I fold the edges of the pancake. Lewis has stopped eating and is watching me.

"When did she get her dog?" he asks.

"Five years ago, when she moved to Marlow. She was twenty-seven." I dip the pancake into plum sauce.

"Did anything else important happen that year?"

"No."

"But she got a German shepherd."

"Lots of people do," I say.

"We found papers in her house. The dog was bred and trained by a security firm in Bristol."

I stop with a spoon halfway to my plate. "What?"

"They sell dogs for protection."

I remember Rachel on the lawn, calling commands while Fenno raced around her. She said she had to train him so he wouldn't be bored. "She told me she adopted him."

"Maybe she was scared," says Lewis, "because of what happened in Snaith."

By the time he finished, she couldn't walk. Every one of her fingernails was split from fighting him.

"Do you think it was him?" I ask.

"I don't know."

"Why would he wait fifteen years?"

"Maybe he was looking for her."

⇥ 6 ⇤

We went to a party the night she was attacked. It was the first week in July and I had a job at the town pool as assistant junior lifeguard, which meant that if three people were drowning at opposite ends of the pool I could rescue the smallest one.

The morning of the party was "a scorcher," according to Radio Humberside. "Be careful out there," the announcer said, which I thought was stretching it. The toast popped up, the electric kettle whistled. I wedged open the sliding door with my foot and ate my breakfast with my back against the glass.

My feet were stretched on the patio stones, and our dad was at work on a building site in Sunderland, the driveway empty of his AMC Gremlin, the world's smallest and ugliest car. Rachel said we were "latchkey children," though technically we weren't since the door was never locked. When I said that, she said, "Stop being stupid."

Rachel was still asleep when I left for the pool. The blind in her room was snagged in one corner and light glowed on her pale arm and dark hair. I closed her door and clattered down the stairs. My dad once asked if I walked down the stairs that way on purpose, to make the maximum possible noise. The screen door slammed behind me and I turned onto the hot, empty street. Half of the houses had been repossessed, and I ambled along the center of the road, brushing the hair back from my face.

After my shift at the pool, I went to Alice's. Rachel met me at the door and I watched her figure take shape beyond the screen.

"How was work, Nora?" asked Alice.

"No drownings."

We left for the party at nine. Rachel walked in front, and Alice and I followed with our arms linked. My sister wore denim shorts and a loose navy shirt. She had sandals that tied at the ankle and a rope bracelet around her wrist, her hair loose down her back. We had poured vodka into a Coke can and walked sipping from it, and all the alcohol floated to the top so by the time we reached the house we were drunk.

When we arrived at the party, everyone began hugging everyone else, including some of the people who had already been there together when we arrived. Rafe pulled me under his arm into the kitchen and I drank another vodka Coke, then another.

I lost Rachel. We played Nevers but no one could remember the rules, and then Rachel came in from the kitchen and squeezed beside me on the sofa. I tipped my head against her shoulder and smelled that she had just smoked a cigarette. I lifted her hair and held it across my nose, breathing through it like a screen.

It gets fuzzy after that.

I remember emptying an ice tray into a cup, then knocking it to the floor, and being on my knees, one hand scrabbling under the fridge.

More people coming.

Another vodka Coke.

Rachel in the kitchen, her hair tied up in a high knot, drinking a glass of water and talking with Rafe. Her knobby cheekbones, her pink lips.

I was swampy with tiredness, and knocking into things. I climbed the stairs, which was interesting because I couldn't see below my knees.

I closed my eyes. And then someone was leaning over me in the earliest light of morning, when it's uncanny, almost neon. I was in a single bed, sleeping on my side next to Alice.

"Nora, I'm going to walk home. Do you want to come with me or stay?" Rachel's hand on my arm.

"Stay." And I nestled against Alice's shoulder and fell back asleep.

The thing was—that morning—I hadn't even turned over to look at her. I imagined it afterward, over and over. Pushing back on my shoulder, twisting around to see her. Her face would be pale in the neon blue light from outside, her hair swinging forward in two long sheets.

"Never mind. I'll come with you."

⇥ 7 ⇤

The next morning, I head down Cale Street to the aqueduct. The path is thirteen miles long, and my plan is to walk for long enough to clear my head. Last night, at the Emerald Gate, I asked Lewis, "Are you going to look for him?"

"Yes," he said. He might already be in Snaith. I can't imagine how the search will work now, after fifteen years. It was difficult enough in the weeks immediately after the attack.

I duck under a gap in the hedge and emerge onto the aqueduct, at the part of the trail where people bring their dogs after work and at the weekend. My heart skips. Three weeks ago Rachel and I came here with Fenno. We took turns throwing the tennis ball for him, wiping our hands on our jeans. When a Portuguese water dog arrived off Cale Street, Rachel folded in half laughing at Fenno's reaction.

As he bowled over to greet the other dog, Rachel wiped tears from her eyes, her mouth pulled down into a crescent. "He's literally quivering with happiness," I said. "I know," she said, "I know."

Rachel chose the dog for protection. She bought him five years ago, soon after she moved here. Lewis thinks she felt unsafe living alone in the countryside, more exposed than in London. Maybe she thought he would find her.

I walk down the aqueduct away from town. The fuel that's always in my stomach now catches and I am sheeted in flames. I can't hear anything, which I don't notice until I am far past the village and realize my shoes must have been making that sound on the path since I started walking.

I stalk between the farms, the flames rippling over me. The rage doesn't go away. After two or three miles I stop and weep into my hands. I drop to my knees. Even with my legs pressed to the frozen ground, I still burn, the fire bristling off my spine.

On my way back, I come through a copse of hazels and around a bend, and there is a figure on the path in front of me.

As I draw closer, I see that it is a man in a long coat. He has a Staffordshire bull terrier on a lead, which is strange. Most people let their dogs run on the aqueduct. When we are close, the dog trots over to greet me, tugging him nearer. The man smiles. He is bald, with a strong chin and a flattened nose, like a boxer.

He says, "This is Brandy." I hold my hand out for the dog to sniff. She presses her wet nose to it and pain sluices through me. I scratch behind her ears, and her eyes crease and her tail swings back and forth. Even though it's cold, she has been sweating. I can see her pink skin through the damp raked lines of her coat.

The stranger isn't wearing gloves, and his hand on the lead is red and chapped. The slight swell of his stomach presses against his coat.

"Sweet girl," I say to the dog. Her eyes fasten on mine with the attention specific to bull terriers, and I wonder if he attacked me if she would lunge for me or him.

A crow calls from the field, and when he turns toward it, I flip the dog's tag over. Denton. They live on Bray Lane, near the common. I can't tell if he caught me reading it.

"Does she run away?" I ask, and point at the lead.

"No," he says. "A friend of mine let his Staffie off lead and his neighbor shot her."

The dog sniffs my wrist, her eyes wide and a little crossed. "They used to be nanny dogs," I say.

"I know. My friend told that to the police. Nothing happened to the shooter. He wasn't even cautioned."

I recognize the grain reaper in the field next to us and realize how far we still are from town. A mile, at least.

"Are you Nora?" he asks. We've never met before. He has gray stubble and a few deep lines across his forehead.

"Yes."

"We used to see Rachel out here," he says. "I can't believe it."

The dog snaps to attention. I turn to look behind me, but the path is empty.

"I saw her just that morning," he says.

My mouth goes dry. His coat sleeve has a small rip at its hem, did my sister do that?

"Where?"

"At her house. The bath sprang a leak. It had been going for a few days before she noticed. There's a crack halfway across the ceiling."

I straighten. We are alone, between drab, stippled fields. I watch his red hand twist the lead. "And she called you?"

"I'm a plumber. If you need help with the house or anything, let me know," he says. His coat is zipped to his chin, leaving only his hands and head exposed. I check for scratches or bruises, but if he has any they are hidden. "My mum died last year. There's a lot to sort out, I'm happy to help."

He walks away. I start toward Marlow, and once he is out of sight, I run.

My phone doesn't have service until Cale Street.

"Have you interviewed someone named Denton yet?"

"Yes," says Moretti, "Keith Denton." I didn't think he would tell me. I thought police interviews were confidential, and for a moment I wonder whom he has told about speaking with me.

"He was at Rachel's house on Friday."

"I know. One of her neighbors saw his van. We interviewed him at the station on Saturday."

"Why did you let him go?"

"We don't have grounds to arrest him. Our technicians are still performing tests on the van. He's not to leave the area."

"Did you check him for injuries?" Rachel had defensive wounds, and the dog was trained by a security firm. He would have tried to protect her.

"We haven't found any evidence to incriminate him. According to him, Rachel was alive and well when he left her house."

"Where was he between three and four?"

"Resting."

"Where?"

"In his van at the pond. He was up the night before on a job in Kidlington."

"Did anyone see him?"

"We're confirming his movements with witnesses and CCTV."

He must have something to gain from telling me this. It must be a technique. I wonder if he thinks the information will trigger some memory for me. That Rachel met lovers at the pond, maybe, or that the location has some meaning.

"Was he the person watching her from the ridge?"

"Nora, I don't know yet. We'll know more when the results return from the lab."

The high street appears almost preternaturally beautiful and civilized, and I am shaky with relief to not be alone with him anymore.

The yellow awning of the Miller's Arms thumps in the wind. Soft clouds marble the windows of the library. There are a dozen people on the street, and one of them, a woman with dark hair and kaleidoscopic blue eyes, stops in front of me. "Nora. I'm so sorry about your sister."

"Are you from the hospital?" I ask.

She shakes her head. "Do you want to get a cup of tea?"

She smiles and squeezes my arm, and I have the sense that people here will look out for me. We go to the Miller's Arms. She sets the tea in front of me and gives me an encouraging smile. The relief of being with another person, in the warmth of company, sinks me into my chair.

I might have just met her murderer. This knowledge roars in my ears. A few minutes, somewhere safe.

I've only been to the Miller's Arms once before. My drink was pale and frothy and it had a violet floating on its surface. This delighted me. "Bloody hell," said Rachel. Her fish pie arrived with one speckled blue-and-red crab claw pointing from its crust, which mollified her a little. "Does it make up for the violet?" I asked. "No, definitely not."

"I'm sorry," I say now. "I don't remember your name."

She sets her cup down and the clink of it on the saucer is so domestic, so incongruous.

"Sarah Collier. I work at the *Telegraph*."

I notice, with a whip of vertigo, the other people in the room looking at us. I stand and walk out.

Sarah catches me up outside. She left her coat indoors and stands, shivering, in a cream-colored jumper, her hands tucked under her arms. "I'm not going to ask you any questions. I'm just here, if you need to talk."

"I'm not talking to the press."

"Did Alistair tell you to say that?" she asks. "You don't need to listen to everything he says."

I don't want Sarah to know where I'm staying, so I walk toward the common. When I look back, the door to the Miller's Arms is swinging shut behind her. I pass the common and turn down Salt Mill Lane. At the side of the road is a memorial, and my first thought is that it is for Rachel. My hand goes to my mouth. There are candles and piles of pale cut flowers. Then I notice the football jersey pinned to the fence, and a card with the name *Callum* across it.

The small semidetached house behind the

fence looks vacant. Rachel told me he died in September, his family won't have sold it yet. I wait until the lane is empty, then kneel to read some of the cards. The messages show people gripped by his death, and anguished by it. A lot of them describe him as a hero. Either no one knew what he was like, or they knew and didn't care.

➤ 8 ⬅

I am crossing the high street when I see Lewis in the newsagent's shop, speaking with the old man who owns it. I wait for him to come out.

"Is he a suspect?"

"No."

From his shop, Giles has an unobstructed view of the train station. He is also the town gossip, according to Rachel. His shop has longer hours than any other business on the high street, and he knows everyone in town. People confide in him. He asks after illnesses, pregnancies, divorces. I remember, absurdly, that he knows about my breakup with Liam. He got it out of me in the two minutes I spent buying a newspaper and bottle of mineral water at his shop in May.

I consider his view, of the hooked lights on the platform and the station house, then follow Lewis up the high street. We find a bench on the common. The priest is in the church graveyard in his black robe. A cedar elm rises above him, sheltering him under its green tier.

"Do Anglican priests hear confession?" I ask.

"No, not formally. Not like Catholic ones. But it wouldn't be any good if they did, they never tell us anything."

The priest climbs the church steps. For a moment, he seems to be looking at us, then he grasps the iron rings inside the two doors and pulls them shut.

"Does he have to close the doors like that?" says Lewis. "Can't he do one, then the other?"

I stare at the stained glass window above the doors. Across the common, wind rushes through the yews, a vast, maritime sound. The wind grows stronger, and it's like I am on the strand in Edinburgh, near my university.

"A man named Andrew Healy assaulted a teenage girl in Whitley two years ago," says Lewis. "It's six miles from Snaith. Rachel wrote him a letter asking to visit him in prison. He agreed, and she visited him in March."

"Was it him?"

"No. Healy was serving a drugs sentence the summer of Rachel's assault."

"Could he have left?"

"It's a class-A prison. The day of her assault he was on canteen duty. They would have recorded it if he somehow stepped out."

"Did Rachel know that?"

"Healy says he told her it couldn't have been him. Rachel spoke to his solicitor, who confirmed the dates of his sentence."

"Where did she visit him?"

"A prison outside Bristol." Lewis looks embarrassed for me. She didn't ask me to come and wait in the car. She didn't even tell me she'd written him. "Did Rachel ever talk about looking for her attacker?"

"She said she stopped. She said she wanted to forget it ever happened."

Of course that was what she told me. For years I had urged her to stop looking, and at a certain point it must have been easier to lie than to argue.

"When was this?" asks Lewis.

"Five years ago. Is he a suspect?"

"No. Healy's still in prison."

At the Hunters I find the route from her house to the prison. I imagine Rachel in the visitors' room as the prisoners start to file in. I don't know what she planned to say. What abuse she would turn on him.

She wouldn't ask him why he did it. I asked her once and she laughed in my face. "He doesn't get to have a reason," she said. She didn't want to meet him to better understand what had happened. She wanted to punish him.

She told me once how she would go about it. She would correspond with other men in the prison and win them over. During her visit, she would mention their names and say what they were willing to do for her.

I don't know how far she would have taken it. If she would actually convince another prisoner to assault him. I doubt it, but the desired effect would be the same.

It wasn't him. Andrew Healy. They must look alike, though, enough for her to call his solicitor to confirm his story. She might have still threatened him. It wasn't her but he still attacked someone. I can see her walking back to the car, her arms tight around herself, her face hatched open with rage.

She would have stopped in Bristol for a drink. I can see the place too; it would be familiar, a chain she had visited in London or Bath. The Slug and Lettuce, or something like it. She would still have all her plans twisting through her head, and she would drink too much to drive home. I am so certain about this that I start to call every midrange hotel in central Bristol.

"Hello, this is Rachel Lawrence. I want to book the same room as I had on my last visit. Could you check what that is?"

As soon as the clerk says they have no record of a Rachel Lawrence, I hang up and dial the next number, until one says, "Room twelve."

I ask the rate. "That seems like more than last time. Is it a weekend rate?"

"The rate on eight March was also ninety-five pounds."

I have a glow of pride. I've always known her better than anyone else.

➤ 9 ◄

"Nora," said Rachel, "do you want to come with me or stay?"

"Stay." And I fell back asleep. Rachel tripped down the stairs. She said good-bye to Rafe and the others who were still awake, then turned the knob so the screen door wheezed open into the summer air. The sun hadn't risen yet but the pavements were warm, had stayed warm through the night.

Rachel told me this story only once, on the assumption that I would remember every part of it, and she never had to tell it to me again.

She walked with her sandals in her hand. Later, she found out the time of the sunrise that day and decided she must have left Rafe's shortly before five. The sky was an uncanny, electric blue. Soon after leaving, she stepped on a sharp pebble and tied her sandals back on. She seemed to think this part was important. She described it precisely. I don't know if this was because she thought she would have been able to run otherwise.

She said she had a surge of happiness. Instead

of going home, she thought about going to the river to watch the sun rise. She said she felt sorry for the people asleep in their houses, that her life was better and more vibrant than theirs.

She crossed onto our council estate, a spiral of identical white boxes, half of them empty.

A man appeared, walking very quickly between two of the houses toward her and the road. She saw him from the corner of her eye as she passed the strip of lawn. When she turned around, the man wasn't on the road behind her, and she assumed he had gone inside.

Then he appeared two houses ahead of her. He must have doubled back and crossed on the lawns. This second appearance unnerved her. She couldn't decide if it would be better to continue on toward home or run back to town.

The man continued down the lawn and stepped onto the road. He didn't look at Rachel, who was now frozen a few meters behind him.

He started to walk away from her, in the same direction as she had been going. When there were about five meters between them, she took a step forward. She liked that he was in front of her. It made her feel more safe. She decided not to run, she decided it would be better if she could see where he was.

For the rest of the walk home, she would be in earshot of other people's houses. If anything were to happen someone would hear and come outside. If she ran away, he might catch her in the stretch of fields between the estate and town, with no one around them.

Keeping the same distance between them, she made it about half a block.

The man turned around and came toward her. He walked strangely, high on the balls of his feet, with short strides. She started to shout at him. While she shouted, he came closer in quick, jerking steps.

It was meant to frighten him away. She had been told that, we had all been told that. Make a scene, draw attention, make it difficult on him, and he will leave you alone.

It didn't make any difference. As soon as he was near enough, his hand closed around her throat, and he pulled her to the ground by her neck. He kneeled beside her, with his leg blocking his groin. With one hand pinning her neck, he punched her in the stomach and chest and face. She hit and scratched him. When he bent close enough, she tried to drive her fist into his windpipe, but he turned and the blow landed under his jaw. He grabbed her hand in the air and snapped her arm, then trapped it under his knee. He bounced her head against the pavement and her scalp turned wet.

He continued to beat her in the stomach and face. Then he stood on the balls of his feet and looked down at her. She cradled her wet head.

She tried to lie still but her body jerked and convulsed. When the seizing stopped, she crawled to her knees, then to her feet, and the ground wheeled. She backed away, because if she turned around he would return from behind the houses, with his short bobbing steps, and pull her to the ground again.

She shuffled across the road. Her left arm was broken and she held it against her chest. As she retreated, her eyes skipped along the gaps between the houses. She heard herself breathing, rapid inhalations pumping her chest.

⇀ 10 ↽

What happened in Rachel's house on Friday didn't fit with anything outside of it. The professor's house across the road. The neighbor riding her horse. The elm trees, the car in the drive.

It doesn't make any sense. There were people in the village, dozens of them, a mile from where she was killed. When I arrived, the town was quiet, like the snow had already started. I saw a woman leaving the library with a stack of books. A man looking at cakes in the bakery window. One of the village employees lifting a sheaf of papers from the seat beside him and climbing from his van. People maneuvering their cars through the narrow streets, listening to the forecast. It was like something set down on Rachel's house, upending it, while the rest of the town was left untouched.

It doesn't make any sense, except that it has happened before. The rest of a town undisturbed while something is loosed on her.

→ 11 ←

"Was Rachel ever on medication for a mental illness?" asks Moretti. It's midmorning on Tuesday, and on the other side of the door, the incident room is crowded. Moretti appears relaxed, and I hope that means they're making progress.

"No."

"Have you ever been?"

"Yes."

"What for?"

"Depression. I started on a course of Wellbutrin in June."

It all caught up to me, the end of my relationship, every other loss. When I saw myself in a mirror, I looked hunted. I was tired all the time, and often had a rising sense of panic in innocuous places—a cake shop, a museum, the rose garden in Regent's Park.

"Are you still taking it?"

"No. I stopped in October."

"On the advice of your psychologist?"

"She said it was my decision." I was better after Cornwall. I had changed since my first visit to the psychologist's office.

"Why was Rachel unmarried?" he asks.

"She valued other things. Why are you not married?"

"I'm divorced," he says, as though it answers the question. "It sounds like Rachel could be unpleasant."

"I liked that about her."

He smiles, and I have the sense that he agrees with me, and understands her. She matters to him now in a way that's different than with anyone else.

⇢ 12 ⇠

"I'm sorry. I'm so sorry I didn't go with you."

"Don't apologize," she said. She lowered her face and pried her rope bracelet from under the hospital wristband. The pale gold straw was now stiff and rust colored, and she began to work it off with her teeth.

When I first saw her, I started to cry and Rachel tilted her head at me. This was a second shock. Her eyes were so swollen I had thought they were closed and that she was asleep. Her appearance frightened me, like the bashed-up girl was the scary thing instead of what had happened to her.

Her face was swollen and garish. Her mouth was twice its normal size, as though she had drawn around it with lipstick, and both of her eyes were almost hidden under black bulges. Someone had combed her hair, and the comb left raked lines in her scalp. A greasy ointment covered the stitches on her brow and cheek. One arm was folded across her body in a sling.

We were at the hospital in Selby, seven miles from Snaith. "How did you get here?"

"Banged on a door. They wouldn't drive me. They were scared I'd die on the way to hospital and they'd be held responsible. I had to talk to the 999 operator myself, and they wanted me to wait for the ambulance outside."

A couple, the same age as our dad, and, she said, with the same habits. "Which house?" I asked, because I was going to torch it when I got home. She couldn't remember the number.

"Has the hospital told Dad?"

"No. I said he was camping."

Two tall men came into the room. Both ignored the visitors' chairs and stood at the end of her bed. Rachel turned her battered head at them, and they asked me to leave. They didn't try to shut the door. If they had, I would have screamed the place down.

She told the officers what she had told me, and she added that the man had black hair to his jaw and a narrow face, with a pronounced plate of bone under his forehead. He wore a canvas jacket that was too large for him. One of the detectives stopped her. "Where had you been?"

"A friend's house."

"And what were you doing out so early?"

"I wanted to go home."

"Had you been drinking?"

"Yes."

"How many drinks did you have?"

I begged her to lie. "Four," she said, and in the hallway I dropped my head to the wall and sighed. It was a lie. It was probably the number she thought reasonable. They were cops, surely they drank, surely they understood that four drinks over many hours wouldn't impair your judgment.

"Anything else?" asked the same officer. The second one was silent. I don't think I heard his voice once.

"What do you mean?"

"Any drugs?"

"No."

"Did you argue with anyone at the party?"

"No."

"How clear is your memory of the night?"

"It's clear."

"Did you recognize this man?"

"No."

"Any chance you saw him before, even in passing?"

"No."

"Do you have a boyfriend?"

"He wasn't my boyfriend. I'd never seen him before."

"It would be helpful if you could answer the question."

"No."

"Can you tell us who was at the party?"

They asked her to go through it a few more times, and then to sign a statement. They said they would be in touch if they identified a suspect, but of course they never did.

⇥ 13 ⇤

Rachel went to Bristol Prison. She would have dressed for the occasion, I think, to prove he didn't damage her. It would be much worse for him than her, in the end. Dark fabric, sharp boots, lipstick. She would dress like her own solicitor.

On the drive to Bristol, the hour and a half on the M4 in March, I imagine she was taut and icy with fury, and triumphant.

"I found you. I always knew I'd find you."

I wonder if she had a few searing minutes of thinking it was finally over before Healy explained he'd been in prison that summer. It's difficult for me to think about. The drive to Bristol is better.

· · ·

"We'll try to finish this as quickly as possible," says Lewis after he joins us in the interview room. "It's unusual for someone like Rachel to be the victim of two random assaults."

"What do you mean, someone like her?"

"Not a sex worker," says Moretti.

"She also lived in areas with a low incidence of violent crime," says Lewis. "She had no involvement in gangs or drugs."

I don't correct him. He means the trade, not snorting lines at a club in Shoreditch. Which I miss, suddenly. I used to wear a pair of ankle boots with a sharp heel, leather leggings, a black cotton shirt that I bought for one million pounds at All-Saints on the King's Road.

I let my head tip back. Rachel liked a club behind Hoxton Square the best. "Let's go take a few dances," she said, and unlatched the toilet stall, and out we went, tripping up the stairs to the main floor.

Across the table, the detectives wait. Rachel rubbed her finger above her sharp white teeth. She rolled a note against her leg.

Moretti unbuttons his suit jacket and leans forward. "Grievous bodily harm," he says in his Scottish accent, "is very similar to murder. It becomes murder if the victim dies. Your sister was the victim of two nearly identical crimes." He stumbles on the last four words, intentionally, I think, to stress how difficult this is to believe. "We'd like to ask you some more questions about the first incident. Can you describe her assailant?"

"He was older than her, around twenty-five, six foot, dark hair, pale, a narrow face with a high, strong forehead. Do you think it was him?"

"He may have been angry that she got away," says Lewis.

"She didn't get away. She could barely walk when he finished."

"Did he rape her?"

"No."

"Why did the attack stop?" asks Lewis.

"She didn't know. He may have thought someone saw them, or he just decided he was done. She said he lurched off her and walked away."

Short bouncing steps. I could imitate him for them, like Rachel did for me, but there isn't any point.

"He walked funny," I say. "On his toes."

Moretti writes this down. The fluorescent lights hum above us. She isn't coming back. Lewis notices me rubbing my head and stands to switch off the lights. The electric whine disappears, and the room dims. Rain patterns the window as the worst of my headache drains away.

Moretti opens a folder and says, "For the purpose of the tape, I am now showing Miss Lawrence three photographs. Do you recognize any of these men?"

"Yes." Both detectives tense. I tap the middle photograph.

"How?" asks Moretti.

"He killed a girl in Leeds."

"Did you ever discuss this man with Rachel?"

"Yes. I showed him to Rachel and she said it wasn't him."

"When?"

"A long time ago. Rachel might have been eighteen or nineteen. I know he was caught right away. He had blood on him and he took the girl's bracelet."

"Why did you show his picture to Rachel?"

"I thought she would want to know."

"But you were surprised that she visited Andrew Healy," says Moretti.

"I was surprised that she visited him in March of this year. She said she wanted to forget about it, and I thought she had."

We were on a trip to Rome, visiting a lemon grove outside the city. "You were right," she said. She scratched her fingernail across the skin of a lemon and sniffed it. "It's time to stop." That night we feasted on pasta and wine. A celebration. I thought it was finished.

"Five years ago, she told me she would stop looking."

"What form did looking take?" asks Moretti.

"We read the newspapers." We read about every rape, assault, and murder in Yorkshire, including ones from the recent past. It did my head in. I won't take cabs alone because of one story. "And in the beginning we also went into Leeds and Hull."

"Why?"

"He might have come on the train."

"Did you think that or did Rachel?"

"She did, I think."

"Do you know why?"

"No. Who are the other two men?"

"Actors," says Lewis. "It's a photographic lineup."

"Why did you think it was that man?" I ask.

"He left Whitemoor Prison three weeks before Rachel's death," says Lewis. "The way he killed the young woman in Leeds is similar to the first attack on Rachel, and at the time of Rachel's assault, he was living in Hensall, near Snaith."

"No," I say. "He didn't attack her then."

They continue to interview me about the assault. They ask about the people we knew, even after I tell them that Rachel could see his face during the attack and was certain she didn't recognize him. Andrew Healy must look similar to him, though she would have accounted for the possible changes in fifteen years, how his face might thin or thicken, and age. They take notes. I think of the sort of police officers who hold press conferences during a major inquiry, and wonder if any of them would have solved this already.

⇒ 14 ⇐

Our dad was not camping, but staying with a friend in Sunderland who had helped him get a job on a building site. When I finally spoke with him on Rachel's third day in hospital, I told him she had broken her ankle. "Can you call Selby Hospital and say she's fine to leave with her sister? Here's the number."

This shouldn't have worked, but it was a crowded NHS hospital and they probably needed her bed.

On Rachel's last day in hospital, Alice borrowed her mum's car and we drove to pick her up. On the return trip, Rachel was quiet, and I wondered if despite what she'd said she was scared to come home.

Alice and I had spent the morning preparing. We rented six films. We bought two pints of wonton soup and chow fun. We drove to the Italian café in Whitley for a quart of hazelnut ice cream. I bought a bottle of cleaning fluid—not the sort of thing in supply at our house—and scoured the bathtub. I had the idea that Rachel, who had never done so before, might want to take a bath. And, in a stroke of genius, we borrowed a friend's dog, a cream-colored Labrador retriever puppy.

Rachel didn't even ask whose it was. It was the

wrong kind of dog, I realized later. Not a Doberman pinscher, for example. We could have tried to borrow one of those, there were plenty in Snaith and on the farms around it. When she saw the dog, she must have realized how little the two of us understood.

Rachel moved slowly up the stairs and into bed. The blind was still snagged up in one corner, and golden afternoon light glowed on her arm. She scrabbled her hand for the duvet and pulled it to her chin. I lay beside her but faced the room, the heaps of clothes, the stacks of books, the empty bottles of Jamaican beer, packs of cigarettes, and scorched lighters. Her mirror leaned on the floor, and next to it were a radio and a few gold tubes of lipstick.

The room was messy but still somehow spare. She didn't curate it for anyone else, and unlike me she didn't display mementos. No matchboxes unless she needed matches. The only wall decoration was a carnival mask with a nose curved like a beak that she had found on a road in Leeds, abandoned, probably, after a party.

I wondered what she made of it now. She hadn't seemed to look at the room at all on her way to bed. We lay with our heads turned in opposite directions on the pillow and listened to the dog whining downstairs.

Soon after leaving hospital, Rachel bought a blackjack from Rafe's older brother. God knows where he got it. It was a small metal rod, like a police baton but smaller. "If it's what the police use instead of a gun, it has to be one step down from a gun, doesn't it?" she asked.

That first night, Alice made us hazelnut milk shakes, which we drank while watching an animated film about foxes. Rachel said she wasn't hungry because of the pain medicine. She twitched often. None of us looked at one another, or at the door, or the window. We kept our eyes on the small screen as night fell.

The next day, she said, "I'm going to Hull. Do you want to come?"

"Why?"

"I need to do some shopping."

Rachel had never, to my mind, needed to do any shopping. For one thing, she didn't have any money.

We rarely went to Hull. We went to Leeds more often, to the Warehouse, the Garage, the Mint Club. During the day, we bought kebabs and merguez rolls and watched the university students in the main square.

It was not, I thought, what Rachel should be doing at the moment. She should be resting. She had not taken a bath yet.

I followed her around Hull, into betting shops, into pubs. People stared at us. She still had her stitches in, and her face was bruised and swollen.

When the train conductor asked what had happened, I waited for her to lie and say a road accident. Instead she said, "I was beat up. He is about six feet tall, has black hair to his chin, and was wearing a canvas jacket. He has a long narrow face and you can see the bones in his forehead." She ran her finger up the edge of her forehead to demonstrate and then wrote something on the back of her ticket receipt and gave it to the conductor. "This is my number, if you see him."

We spent the entire day in Hull, and the next, and then we went to Leeds. These trips were excruciating. Rachel still couldn't walk without pain. Watching her limp in and out of shops and pubs filled me with a pity that made it difficult to breathe.

I knew we wouldn't find him, and on the return trip we were both frustrated and miserable. She spent the walk home from the train hoping we'd see him, and I spent it begging that we wouldn't.

The police did not help. Rachel went to the station and spoke to a detective constable who spent the entire interview asking her for information about the flow of drugs into Snaith. Aside from his face, the only thing Rachel had to go on was that she thought she heard his voice. His accent sounded like ours, she said. He was local.

We assumed he was poor, because we were, and he was in our town. We went to the places our father would go. The tracks. The pubs. Where would a violent man go, where would a monster go. It was hard to know what someone who liked hurting women would also like.

→ 15 ←

The body of the missing woman I heard about on the day of Rachel's death was found this morning in the River Humber. Nicole Shepherd. Divers were in the river examining the posts of the bridge at Hessle, which is overdue for repairs, and they found her body in a sleeping bag weighted with breeze blocks. Whoever it was threw her from the center of the bridge, but the river isn't very deep by Hessle, only thirty feet, and the current isn't strong.

My stomach twists while I read the rest of the article, hunched in my coat at one of the tables outside the inn, holding the paper down with my forearms against the wind. Of course she came to harm. I wonder if they can figure out who owned the sleeping bag.

The bell over the newsagent's door peals and I look up. I wait for a moment, and then I lift my hand to wave.

Keith unties his dog's lead and crosses the road toward me. His shadow spills over the table and I look up at him, shading my eyes with my hand. He wears the same coat as on the aqueduct, but open, with a work shirt underneath. He is solid and tall but soft at the middle.

"Hello," I say. I fold the newspaper and stow it on the bench beside me.

"Are they treating you well?" he asks, pointing at the inn.

"Yes."

He nods. The silence stretches and I slip my hand inside the paper for comfort. The sound of a sledge-hammer comes from behind the inn, and Keith says, "They've been repairing that road for weeks."

The dog rests her front paws on my lap, and I scratch behind her ears. She presses her head against my chest. Keith says, "Nice to see you again. If there's anything we can do." He steps back, pulling on the dog's lead so she drops from the bench and out of my reach.

"Actually," I say, and he stops. "I've just had a phone call. The police are done with Rachel's car. It's at a place in Didcot, and there aren't any buses to it."

He stares at me as though he doesn't under-stand. I wait, and then he says, "Not a problem. I can take you now if you like."

In my room, I pack the carving knife, wrapped in a leather glove, and a can of pepper spray. On my way out the door, I tell the manager that Keith Denton is giving me a lift to Didcot. She smiles and says, "How nice of him."

Keith arrives in a black Renault. "Not the van," I say as I climb in.

"Only for jobs. It uses too much fuel."

I grip the can of pepper spray in my pocket. Both of his hands hold the wheel. I expected to be scared but instead I'm filled with anticipation, and a rising sense of power. He's nervous.

We drive through Marlow. The door next to me is unlocked, and I roll the window down. The day is bright, and he doesn't comment on the cold draft. He asks if we have any family in the area, and I say no. He switches on the radio. I direct him onto the motorway. As he pulls onto the slip road, I say, "It must be especially difficult for you."

"Why?"

"You saw her right before it happened."

His hands roll forward on the wheel, then back. If you did it, I think, I will destroy you. He leans from his seat, checking the next lane with exaggerated care before merging.

He doesn't speak for a long time, and then he says, "He might have already been there, waiting for me to leave. I should have noticed."

"This is the exit," I say. We drive past a parade of shops, a shipping depot, a storage facility. He drives slowly, checking the numbers on the side of the road. There isn't any foot traffic and for the first time since we left I'm frightened.

"Here."

He pulls into the lot, where a guard sits in a

booth at the entrance. Keith passes my license through the window to him, and we wait in silence as he searches for my record. Keith appears restless, and I wonder if he came here to collect his van after it was tested for her blood.

The guard returns my license and the gate swings open. Keith starts driving down the first row. I scan the cars, and then he stops. I look past him at Rachel's car, an old Jeep. He turns to me with his mouth compressed in a tight smile, waiting for me to go.

"Thank you. Are you hungry?" I ask. "Can I take you someplace?"

We agree to meet at the Duck and Cover. After he leaves, I lock her car around me. The interior smells familiar, warm and dusty. I open the glove box and take out a small gold tube of lipstick. The color, when I open it, is a vivid dark red.

She had so much left to do. It isn't that she had something grand in mind, at least not that I know of. It is worse than that, she has been taken away from everything, she lost everything. She likes red lipstick, and will never again stand in the aisle at a chemist's, testing the shades on the back of her hand. She likes films, and will miss all the ones coming out at the holidays that she planned to see. She likes pan con tomate, and will never again come home from work and mash tomatoes and garlic and olive oil, and rub it onto grilled bread, and eat it standing in her kitchen.

• • •

At the Duck and Cover, Keith orders a whisky. The disappointment makes me slump. They carry Tennent's, the same green cans of lager as the ones on the ridge.

"Miss?"

"A Tennent's, please." I point at the can. Keith doesn't react. The bartender sets down our drinks and leans against the bar with his back to us, arms folded, watching greyhounds pelt down a track.

"Do you usually drink whisky in the daytime?" I ask.

"No," says Keith, watching the dogs.

"What's your usual?" I say it loudly, hoping the bartender will correct him if he lies.

"I don't have one."

The greyhounds disappear into mist. The race ends, and a photograph shows the distance between the front two dogs' noses and the finish line. Their noses are very long, like horses'.

"Anything to eat?" asks the bartender.

"I'm not hungry," says Keith.

"No, me neither."

The bartender takes a pack of Benson and Hedges from a shelf and goes onto the back patio, leaving the door cracked open. If I shout, he will come back inside. I don't know which of the two men would be stronger. I swallow a long draft of beer and wish it were whisky.

"You were eager to help," I say.

Keith doesn't straighten or look at me, but something in him tenses and flexes.

"Rachel was lovely. She was a lovely woman."

"Did you fancy her?"

"I'm married." I shrug. He says, "No, it's not like that."

"What was it like?"

"With Tash? It's good. It's normal."

"No, with Rachel."

He sets down his whisky and I think he's going to hit me. "I barely knew her."

Nothing happens, but I am sure he wanted to strike me. "I didn't tell you when to stop," I say, and he watches me. "How did you know which car was hers?"

"I'd just done a job at her house."

"Rachel told me you were obsessed with her."

He puts a note on the bar and leaves. I can't tell if it was the right thing to say. She never mentioned him.

⇒ 16 ⇐

Moretti calls. "We're done with the house. Let me give you the number of a cleaning agency."

"You don't handle that?"

"No."

"Do you pay for it?"

"No."

"We don't have to clean it. If it will compromise evidence—"

"We have what we need," he says, and I take down the number. The agency is called Combe Cleaners. You wouldn't know their specialty unless you asked. "You'll want to have the cleaners in before you go back," he says. "We can arrange for people to be at the house when you arrive, light a fire, make sure the boiler is on. Some families like to have a priest bless the house. Should I arrange anything like that?"

"What people?"

"Friends of yours and Rachel's."

"Oh." I thought he meant strangers, or guards, which I would have preferred. "No, thank you."

I decide not to wait for the cleaners.

A few yellow leaves hang from the elms on either side of Rachel's house. Some noise flushes the birds from the trees and they wheel into the sky. The air smells of water and mud and hay and the smokiness that courses over the countryside in November. Across the road, Rachel's neighbor rides in her paddock on the same dappled horse as on the day Rachel was killed.

Smoke rises from the chimney at the professor's house. Two cars are parked in its open barn. Wind flattens the thorn trees on top of the ridge and bends the column of smoke until it is almost horizontal.

When I open the door, I think someone else is inside. I have a sense of the pressure changing, a floorboard lowering. I wait on the step, listening, but I don't hear another creak, or a door close.

I can't do this. The blood staining the floors and the walls has turned black. My ears start to ring. But she might have left something inside about Keith, or someone following her, or her friend from the hospital.

I raise the thermostat, and there is a roar as the boiler comes on in the basement. My whole body twitches at the sound. I look at the banister. The dog's lead didn't cause any damage, and in the row of four turned wooden posts the one he hanged from doesn't look different from the others, except for a few stains. I think, nonsensically, of the houses on Priory Walk in Chelsea, the identical white decoys on either side.

I check the ceiling, and it does have a long crack across it. Keith was telling the truth about that much. The radiators start to hiss as I cross the living room. Anything important will probably be in the files under her desk, but I decide to start downstairs. I move through the rooms, looking for anything out of order, anything the police might have missed.

All the surfaces are covered with a thin layer of black carbon. I run my finger through it and sniff, but it doesn't smell like anything. The police also left ice in the sink in the kitchen, though other than that the room is unchanged. The pot on the hob. The slate bowl of chestnuts.

Her ax is propped against the back door. The sight of it prompts a burst of hope, as though she has a chance now.

I imagine coming in with a fire lit, and the living room filled with people, and someone cooking dinner in the kitchen, and the lamps burning against the dreck. It wouldn't have made it easier. I imagine a priest walking through the rooms, reading a psalm, but the only lines that come to mind are from a poem. *And I have asked to be / Where no storms come.*

Through the front window, I look across the valley until I think I find the hole cut in the trees. He might have come in the house on one of the days he watched her. She left a key under the mat, he could have let himself in when she was at work or asleep. I try not to think of it. I can't decide if I would feel safer with the front door locked or unlocked.

I switch on a lamp and the kitchen glows faintly, with the drizzle at the windows. The round wooden table near the entryway, the rag rug, the oven across the room. A thick bunch of parsley stands in a glass of water by the sink. On the shelf above it is a package of pasta striped pink and green, shaped like tricorner hats. Rachel had an alert on tickets to Rome, and I imagine the travel deals still filing into her in-box, unread messages ticking in one by one.

I open the cupboards, which smell, as they always have, faintly of incense, and stare at the boxes of tea, bags of lentils, flour, the jars of sherbet lemons and wine gums and licorice ropes. A few weeks ago, we came back from the cinema and she walked to the counter, where the jar of licorice stood empty.

"Was this you?" she asked.

"Oh, sorry," I said. She hadn't even taken off her coat, she walked straight to the counter and pointed at the jar with her gloved hand. I can't remember if she sounded scared, or just annoyed at me for finishing it. It was a strange way to phrase it, I realize now. Who else could it have been?

As I leave the kitchen, I stumble. My hearing tunnels, then disappears, and my vision breaks into spots like pixels. I lean my forehead on the counter until I can hear the wind gusting around the house again, and the slush of a car driving by, and myself sighing.

I am going up the stairs, and then for a long time I am staring at her handprint on the steps. I can see the notches in her fingers and the three deep lines across her palm.

I hold on to the banister, then tip forward onto the step. I crawl up the stairs and the corridor stretches dim and empty in front of me. Past the open doors, the other rooms are bathed in pale light. I press myself flat to the floor where I last saw her. I don't think I'll be able to get up again. I think of her socked feet.

Her bedroom still smells like her. Across the valley, the red light on the radio tower has a foggy halo. The radiators hiss steam into the room.

Her desk has two filing cabinets underneath it, and I start to sort through the papers. Someone may have written to her. She was clever. If she knew she was being stalked, she would keep a record of it.

Stacks of bureaucratic papers, from the hospital, from the bank, from the purchase of her home. Old letters, recipes, lists of projects around the house. It takes a long time to go through all of it, and I find nothing, no mention of Keith, or someone named Martin, no suspicious notes or letters.

In the bathroom there is a jar of olive oil and sea salt. My heart lurches. It seems an impossible thing for her to have done. Who has the time? Though it doesn't take any, of course, pouring a thick cup of olive oil and stirring in the salt. The jar is the same brown as the bottle of hydrogen peroxide next to it, which she used on cuts and to dry the water in her ears after swimming.

She was moving to Cornwall, five hours away. I wonder if that would have been far enough. It felt safe, though. All those small villages. The walls of trees. Smugglers hid there for centuries. St. Ives is large, too, she could blend in.

At the Chinese restaurant, I asked Lewis why it would take the man who attacked her in Snaith so long to find her. "He might not have known her name," he said.

I wonder if Rachel thought she was about to lurch out of the house, call for help, survive. If as she died, she was thinking, On the count of three—

There are two full suitcases in the boot of her car. She had started to pack for Cornwall.

→ 17 ←

I was on the cliff path in Polperro. There were beach roses. I was hauling groceries to our house. Bottles of tonic, cherries, potatoes, spinach, crisps, lemons, and a dozen channel scallops. The shop in town sold ice and firewood. All the grocer's shops in Cornwall sold ice and firewood.

The bottles of tonic knocked against my knees. Below the cliff, a fishing boat motored through a cloud of seagulls. It looked talismanic, with the birds whirling around it, but, then, so did a lot of things here, like the pointed white caps on the dock pilings, and the anchor ropes disappearing under water.

We ate dinner together every night in Cornwall and had an endless number of things to say. She was my favorite person to talk with, because what caught her attention caught mine too. Rachel cooked and I did the shopping, which I didn't mind. I liked seeing all the boats straining in the same direction in the harbor and the traps stacked on the quay.

I was starving. We both were, all the time. "Sea air," said Rachel. I went to the grocer's nearly every day to replenish our stocks. I wanted salt and vinegar crisps, which tasted like seawater, and Rachel wanted pots of toffee. "What has toffee got to do with the ocean?" I asked, and she said, "It's delicious."

I carried the groceries down the path. The beach roses were pink and the Kilburn high street was hundreds of miles away. Later, after I unpacked the groceries, the sun sank through bars of gray cloud, lighting a red path on the water. "The sun road," said Rachel.

⇥ 18 ⇤

On my way back from her house, the priest stops me and introduces himself. He is only in his thirties and reminds me of the boys I went to school with at St. Andrews. Who knows how he ended up here. He should be banking.

He asks about arrangements for the funeral. "They won't let me bury her," I say. We stand by the rill, a thin, decorative stream that runs down Boar Lane between the houses and the road. He tells me we can still hold a funeral and offers to perform the service.

"She wasn't religious. She thought all religions are cults and some, like yours, are just better at distracting people from the fact that they're cults."

"I can lead a secular service," he says. His willingness to please unnerves me. It isn't what I expect from a priest. "Has it come to that, then?" I ask, and he toes a pebble into the rill. We both watch it sink. He says, "I want to help, and I think a funeral is necessary. To honor her. We have room for one hundred people. Do you want to come inside and see?"

Dust, wood, winter sunlight, black-mullioned windows, the smell of candles like the wax my flatmate in Edinburgh melted down to make encaustic for paintings. An Anglican church. We never had to go when we were children, so it only reminds me of weddings, and Anne Boleyn.

"This would be fine," I say.

As we sit in the front pew of the empty church, planning the service, he says, "I did know her."

"Did you?"

"She sometimes dropped Fenno with me."

I realize he must not have much to do, that he

91

must be lonely. I picture him chattering to Fenno while they walk and think my heart will break.

We place phone calls. Before calling Helen, I go into the garden and pace along the church wall. Rachel was her best friend and her daughter's godmother.

Helen has always made me nervous. She moved from Melbourne to Oxford when her daughter, Daisy, was an infant, and raised her on her own while training and then working as a nurse. The thought of Helen maintaining a household, heating infant formula after a shift, dropping her daughter at nursery and picking her up, always made me feel useless. I don't think I would be able to manage either one, let alone both, and Helen seems to agree.

When she answers, her voice sounds stiff. We discuss the police inquiry, and she agrees to do the eulogy. After a pause, I say, "How did Rachel seem last week?"

"Fine, a little withdrawn. She said work was trying."

"Why was she staying with you?"

"Her boiler was broken," she says. "She had no heat."

Rachel lied to her. I would have noticed if the house were cold on Friday.

"Did she tell you she was moving?" I ask.

"No. To where?"

"Cornwall. She would have been there by now."

"No, that's not possible. She didn't give notice."

"Who do you think did it?" I ask.

"I don't know." She pauses. "It might not have had anything to do with Rachel. It might have been the location."

"What do you mean?"

"It's secluded. Close to a major motorway. Where was she moving in Cornwall?"

"St. Ives."

"I thought she liked the Lizard."

"We've been there. She wouldn't go to a place she'd been if she wanted to get away from someone. Has she ever mentioned a man named Keith Denton to you?"

"No."

"Are you certain?"

"Yes. Do you really think that's why she wanted to move? Cornwall isn't very far, it's only five hours."

"It feels farther," I say. "And it's not so easy to find someone. If she changed her name."

"I doubt she thought she was in danger. She would have reported it."

"Someone was watching her from the ridge by her house."

I can tell Helen doesn't believe me. When I return inside, the priest says, "Did you have any music in mind?"

"Gymnopédie number one."

He says he will locate a piano player.

"Do people tell you their secrets?" I ask.

"Sometimes."

"If one of your parishioners told you they had done something wrong, what would you do?"

"I don't know," he says. "It would depend on the severity of the transgression."

My friends start to arrive at the Hunters on the day before the funeral. This alarms me. I thought they would all stay in Oxford.

I sit on the landing, out of sight, and listen to them bumping into each other. Despite the circumstances, there is something giddy about the encounters, like it's a reunion or a wedding.

"I didn't know you were coming," I hear them say, again and again.

I recognize the voices downstairs, but without any sense of possession. I can't claim any of them and, hunched on the steps, I'm surprised I ever could.

Then Martha is coming up the stairs at a run. Before I can say anything, she is on the landing and her arms close around me.

On the night before her funeral, I can't sleep. The dread grows worse with every hour and warps the next day into something I won't survive without rest. I don't have sleeping pills or tranquilizers, but I do have the bottle of red wine I brought from London for Rachel. There isn't a corkscrew in the room. I go downstairs, but the heavy wooden doors to the bar are locked. Upstairs, I stare at the bottle of red wine. I use a knife to cut the foil and then consider the cork.

There is a screwdriver on top of the bathroom cabinet. Someone must have forgotten it after a repair.

I dig the screwdriver into the cork, pushing it down the neck of the bottle. There is a crash as the cork breaks the seal and wine erupts. Red liquid gushes onto my stomach and drips down my chest.

I sit with the screwdriver in my hand. The wine tracks down my arms along my veins. The wet plasters my shirt to my stomach. There are red spatters on the walls, and already the room smells rancid. I stay where I am, under the stained walls, as the ringing starts in my ears, and grip the screwdriver.

➤ 19 ◄

Before the funeral starts, I scan the church and kill each person in exchange for her. They stand three deep behind the benches and along the walls. I recognize some of them from the library, the pubs, the aqueduct. I notice Lewis and Moretti and the woman, the DCI who walked up the hill with Moretti that day. They sit apart, which at first I think is a tactical police maneuver, but is probably only because they arrived separately and the church filled quickly.

Our dad has not turned up. As far as I know, the police have not found him yet, but this is the funeral of his eldest daughter. He might learn of it somehow. He might limp up the aisle and settle in next to me and start to offer theories. The church doors are shut now, and I wonder if anyone would mind if I locked them.

There are too many people I don't recognize, which I hadn't expected. I thought I would be able to note any strangers. Whoever did it might come today.

I find Keith Denton in the crowd. Lewis has him in view, across the aisle, and I'm glad since I can't watch him myself. A dark-haired woman sits in the rear bench, and I turn to Martha. "There's a journalist here," I say, pointing to her.

Martha clips down the aisle until she reaches the last row. After some discussion, the journalist stands, squeezes past the others on her bench, and leaves through the main doors of the church. Before she does, she gives me a wry smile, like we are in on a joke together. She doesn't show any embarrassment, even as the church turns to stare at her, and I envy her. She seems free.

Stephen has arrived, I realize with a sort of terror. He comes up and kisses me on the cheek. He smells of whisky, and from this morning, not last night.

People shift aside to allow him to rest against the wall. He looks exhausted, and I wonder if he also keeps needing to sit down.

They almost got married. Close brush, she said. He still wanted to. They slept together a few times a year, and he thought she would change her mind and move to Dorset with him. She might have done, eventually. She did love him.

I glance at him. His position or balance is wrong, like he might slide off the wall. Moretti said he was at his restaurant, but I wonder if he has proof.

The air in the church is restive and tortured, the result of two hundred people trying not to make a sound. I wish they would all talk. Outside, through the side door, is the garden. There's still snow in the shade of the church, and under the cedar elms, and the air this morning is clear and scouring.

The priest climbs to the lectern. His sermon and the eulogy are wrong. They're laughable. I look at Stephen and know he agrees. I wish I had done it myself, though even now I'm crying too hard to speak.

The piano player sets up her music, and I watch, already disappointed. She's too young, for one thing.

The song starts and it's like a rope is cut. Something washes over the crowd, settling it. The song isn't sad, which is why listening to it agonizes me, and Stephen, I can tell. The point is that she loved it, and she can't hear it.

Neither of the town's pubs is big enough for us, so the group splits. Without discussion, the out-of-towners go to the Miller's Arms, and the locals to the Duck and Cover. There are a few exceptions. Stephen goes to the Duck and Cover. He walks alone from the church to the pub and looks set on destroying himself. None of the detectives come to the reception. They climb into separate cars and drive back toward Abingdon.

At the Miller's Arms, I carry my glass of whisky around the room from group to group. People watch me. Most of the guests apologize for my loss, and then leave me to steer the conversation somewhere else, which I can't. My wet eyes give the room facets and panels that it doesn't have. I notice with surprise that everything that has always been difficult about parties is still difficult. I go to the toilet eight times and for a cigarette three times.

I am surprised that Liam didn't come, but of course Martha wouldn't have invited him. Why would she, we aren't together anymore. I think of the song he always played in the beginning. Never a frown with golden brown.

Daisy, Rachel's goddaughter, finds me smoking under the awning. She wears a coat over a thin black matelot top and black jeans. She hugs me and says, "I miss her," and I nod, my chin pushing into her shoulder.

They had an arrangement. If anything happened to Helen, Rachel would take in Daisy. Part of me expected it to happen. When Daisy was younger, I thought that if Rachel had to adopt her, I would move in to help, and the thought of that sort of responsibility excited me.

"Rachel would want you to have something of hers," I say.

"What?"

"I've no idea. Why don't you go to her house and pick something?"

We go back into the pub. No one wants to talk about what happened, or how I found her. They seem to think it morbid to describe the sequence of events, that I should want to talk about Rachel's life, which I do, desperately. But I want to talk about this too, with someone who isn't a policeman. I wish I could tell Rachel, she would want to know every part of it.

I go to the toilet again. As I walk back to the bar, I notice that the crowd has thinned. I let my head fall. Martha steers me outside. We don't speak, and I lean against her as we make our way down the high street.

In my room, I wipe the makeup from my eyes and lips and throw the stained pads in the bin. Martha climbs into bed. She sets a pillow down the middle, like she did on trips at university, and says, "It's for your own protection. I'll break your face if you try to steal my blankets."

The dog rotates from the ceiling. I can hear him whining. The fall didn't break his neck and the lead is strangling him. I stand on the bed and reach my arms up. If I can hold him an inch higher he will be able to breathe. I can't get to him, and then he isn't there anymore, and Martha is saying my name.

⇥ 20 ⇤

In the morning, Martha and I sit in our coats at one of the tables next to the inn. She smokes and we watch the trains go by, hard and glinting and mineral in the winter light.

"The lead detective wants to open a fish restaurant in Whitstable," I say.

"What about the other one?"

"He's clever. They're both clever, but I don't know if they're good at their jobs."

In the spring, the Hunters puts up white canvas umbrellas. It was one of the things I always looked for as the train pulled into the station, the four stiff canvas umbrellas, to know I had arrived. Now our table is bare, and I move my coffee cup over the hole at its center.

"Do you want help raising publicity?" she asks.

"No," I say sharply. Martha ashes her cigarette and waits. "The famous ones never get solved."

"Is that true?"

Silence falls as we think about famous victims. I fold my hands in my lap. Clouds drift overhead.

Martha wears a linen scarf and suede boots. To her embarrassment, her family has an estate in Cirencester, with a wine cellar and a gun cabinet. In one of my favorite photographs of her, Martha stands on a hill covered in heather with a rifle broken over her arm.

"Do you want a private investigator?" she asks. "I found one in Oxford with good references."

"No, not yet. I don't want to get in the detectives' way. But I do need to ask you a favor. Can you help me rent out my flat?"

"Are you still not coming back?"

"The police want me to stay in the area."

"For how long?"

"They didn't say." It made sense to me, I hadn't considered leaving. "Rachel said there was something wrong with the town, only a few weeks ago. And she put her house for sale and rented a place in St. Ives. I think she wanted to escape from someone."

"Not necessarily someone from Marlow." At the station, there is a ping and an automated announcement about the London train. We both turn our heads to listen. Martha has to be back in the city soon for a meeting. "How can you afford this?"

"Credit." The gold rooster on top of the inn gleams in the light. My card has a cap of eight thousand pounds. I should open a new one for when I reach the limit.

"Come stay with me," says Martha. I shake my head. "Then I'll come stay here."

"You can't."

"I wouldn't mind leaving for a while."

"Liar."

Martha is acting in a Caryl Churchill play at the Royal Court Upstairs. I saw it at the start of the run early this month. The production is a two-hander and her best role yet.

"No, it's for the best. If I don't live alone now, I'll never be able to again."

Martha leans down to zip her luggage. "Is there something you're not telling me?" she asks.

"No."

She studies the inn, the cream stone and black shutters, and the row of modest houses behind it. In this light, it's difficult to tell if anyone's at home.

"Do you think you know who did it?"

"No."

We sit in silence. Martha smokes, blowing the column to the side. I can tell she doesn't believe me. A train goes by and reflected light bubbles over the wall of the Hunters. "What do you want me to do about the flat?" she asks.

•••

After Martha boards her train, I watch it pull from the station, fighting the idea that I am being abandoned. She appears to be the last of the guests to leave. I thought they would stay longer, and knowing that they didn't is like watching it grow dark in the afternoon.

I have to drop Rachel's keys at the cleaning agency. Afterward, I will take the train to London and clean out my flat. There is nothing else for me to do today, but I still feel breathless and sick, like I've forgotten something important.

Stephen is shoving a bag into the boot of his car in front of the chip shop. There is a moment when we might pretend not to see each other, but neither of us is able to look away in time. As I walk toward him, I stare up the high street to the yellow awning of the Miller's Arms, as though that is my true destination, and I will only be stopping for a moment.

"Are you going home?"

He nods. Stephen lives on the Jurassic Coast, two and a half hours away. They both did the drive so many times. And now it's over. This route they knew so well no longer exists.

And all the landmarks are gone too, the ways she gauged the distance—the spires of towns on the Salisbury Plain, the service station where she always stopped for coffee, the sign for his town, the shapes of his neighbors' houses. Then she was there, opening the car, her feet creaking on the gravel, and pulling her overnight bag over her shoulder, and heading for his door, with exhilaration in the beginning, and a sense of doom around the end of their engagement, and lately, in the past two years, some sensation I could never pin down.

"How's the restaurant?"

Stephen owns a Mexican restaurant in West Bay. Even in the off-season, La Fondita does tremendous business.

"I don't know. Fine. Tom is going to look after it for a while," he says.

He's so handsome. That was part of the problem. Rachel thought he was too lucky. Not anymore. After this, he would be perfect for her. A high, mangled sound leaves my throat.

"I thought your dad would come."

"No." I don't tell him our dad wasn't invited. Stephen never understood about our father. But, then, it isn't an easy thing to understand.

Neither of us knows what to say. I think how strange it is, after how much time we've spent together. A few years ago, the three of us visited Lyme Regis, where the woman who found the dinosaurs lived. I remember being very sad when we went to the dinosaur museum. One of my plays had just been rejected by a competition. I wondered if the woman who discovered the dinosaurs ever found her life as absurd as I found mine.

"She didn't find dinosaurs, Nora, she found fossils," said Rachel. And that was the problem, wasn't it.

Afterward, we sat in front of a pub the color of pistachio ice cream. I got shit-faced on beer, as did Rachel, companionably, and at some point I laughed so hard I fell off the bench. On the drive down the coast, I watched how the cliffs were eaten away into folds, how the grass grew right to their edge, the felt tip of the coast a green curving line. Watching them, my thoughts expanded to a grand scale, consoling me. In the front seat Rachel, also drunk, also watching the pale cliffs and thinking her own noble, magnificent thoughts, held Stephen's hand.

"I miss Rachel." My voice cracks open on her name, like I am yawning.

Stephen looks down the high street, and I am ashamed of saying it. It didn't need to be said. I remember seeing them asleep on his couch. His lips pursed, chin doubled, kissing the top of her head.

"Will you tell me anything the police tell you? I keep calling the station but they won't give me anything."

"Of course."

He closes the boot and comes around to the driver's door. I try to ignore how uneasy he makes me now. The police must have confirmed his story. If he was at work all day, dozens of people saw him. He isn't a suspect. But the police aren't telling him anything.

Stephen takes out his keys and stands looking down at them.

"Was she seeing someone?" he asks.

"No."

"She seemed different the last time I saw her. I wanted to visit in October, and she said she had to work."

"She probably did."

There is a pause, and Stephen's expression shifts. "Did you tell her not to marry me?"

"What, two years ago?"

"Yes, and since."

"Do you think she would have listened to me one way or the other?"

"So you did."

"No." I wonder if he can tell I'm lying. Rachel was restless. I said that if she was restless already, marrying him was probably not the best idea. But she had already decided by then. "I told her she would be fine either way."

"She isn't fine. If we'd married she would still be alive."

"You're right. I wish she had moved to Dorset."

And, a few years later, divorced you. By now she would be starting over somewhere, in a new flat, happily on her own again. Unless neither of us is right, and someone has been following her, and would have found her no matter where she went.

→ 21 ←

At noon, I take the train to London to close my flat. Soon after I leave, a man with the cleaners calls to say they have arrived at the house. While my sister's blood is cleaned from her walls and floor, I watch the view from the train window. Between the snow and the low white clouds are villages of houses with stained yellow roofs, fields, Roman roads.

He said they would sand the floor and then revarnish it. Part of me is relieved—there won't be a trace left of what he did to her—but it also seems strange. Shouldn't we leave it as it is. Or burn the place down.

The thing lodged under my ribs begins to ache. A car with smoke fuming behind it drives alongside the train. Rachel crawls up the stairs. The dog rotates from the ceiling, and blood drips from his paws.

There is a thump and then a suck of air as another train rockets by us. Sounds seem to dwindle into the vacuum between the two trains, and then it has passed and I look out at a stone house with lancet windows.

Keith Denton said that he was resting in his van at the pond during her murder.

The watcher on the ridge drank Tennent's Light Ale and smoked Dunhills.

Rachel decided to leave Oxfordshire.

Stephen is angry she refused him.

I need to know why it happened, so I can stop it from happening. When I opened the door, her house began to shine, and Rachel in my mind began to shine. The way when soldiers go berserk, they recall the battle slowing down, and themselves entranced by it.

I should have made the trip back to London seven days ago, last Sunday night. On Saturday we would have driven into Broadwell for breakfast—lingonberry crêpes, dark coffee—and wandered through the museum. At home, she would have a glass of wine, and I would build a fire or take a bath. On Sunday we would take the dog on the aqueduct, and read, cook lunch, discuss the goats she planned to raise, then I'd head back to London and she'd go to work since she was on the night shift.

I am furious at what has been taken away from us. It is too large to consider all at once, so I focus on smaller things. I want lingonberry crêpes very badly, for example.

The train passes through a village, its steeple sliding by. I look out at the snow, the yellow-gray houses and evergreen trees, the hanging sign of the Mermaid. At the edge of the village is a church with a small graveyard. While the graveyard hovers in front of my window, I count twelve tombstones in the snow, and then the scene begins to drift from view, shaking with the train's movement, and is gone.

I close my eyes, sickened with guilt, horrified at how much better it is to be alive than dead. I swallow, listening to the sound it makes in the back of my throat. If I had been any faster she would be alive.

Land streams by the window. Sheep arranged on the stony flank of a hill, the troubling clouds surging behind it. A firehouse with a man doing exercises in its yard. He pulls himself above a bar, lowers himself, vanishes.

Beside me Rachel is sleeping. If I lean forward, I will see her faint reflection on the window. Her chest rising and falling. The snow, the power lines, and the fences running through her body. Her dark hair pulled over one shoulder, her arms crossed above her stomach. She is wearing a camel-colored sweater. I can see its fibers on the windowpane.

We approach Heathrow. A huge jet glides in to land, its windows a series of yellow drops in the faded light. This used to be the part of the trip when I started to get excited about coming home.

Lately, though, coming back to London has filled me with a sense of doom. I thought about Liam less when I was away. In London, I followed the same routines and visited the same places as when we were together, so it was easy to think that everything was like before, except a little worse.

After Ealing Broadway, the landscape turns modern and industrial. People bundled into winter coats cross the bridges over the tracks. Moretti calls as the train plunges under the Westway flyover. "We have some news," he says. "We located your father."

My skull aches. I thought he was going to say they made an arrest.

"Do you want a number for him?" he asks.

"No. Did you get results back from the materials on the ridge?"

"They couldn't retrieve any DNA evidence."

I dig the heel of my hand into my eye. "None? How is that possible?"

"It's rained quite a lot in the last few weeks."

The train docks in Paddington. I step onto the platform, breathing in the sharp winter air and the familiar ashy, Victorian smell of the station. Patches of snow melt on the glass roof between the iron rafters, and light comes through the glass yellow.

The investigation will not be swift, I realize. The police don't know who watched Rachel. They don't know if Keith is lying. They don't know who attacked her fifteen years ago.

London appears menacing and sinister. No one

knows where I am, and anything could happen. I think uneasily of the canals and the basin. I always thought of myself as safer in London than anywhere else in the world. Each potential assailant was balanced by a potential defender. But horrible things still happen here, and now they might rise up and envelop me.

It begins to rain as I come up from the tube station in Maida Vale, and I shake open my umbrella, surprised to find it still at the bottom of my bag, where I put it when I left my flat nine days ago. I look at the concrete under the edge of my umbrella, then tilt its brim back so I can see down the road. For a moment as the brim rises, I am in the old London, mysterious and cinematic, the finials of umbrellas moving up and down around me, the rain dashing on the road.

The air is cool and fresh and tarry. My legs are already damp and my jeans cling to my skin. I turn to look in the window of a pie shop. Four and twenty blackbirds. Rachel had an enamel black-bird. I remember her sinking its pin into a pie crust. In Cornwall we saw pies with fish heads cooked in honor of the sailor Tom Bawcock. I wonder when Rachel and I will go back to Polperro, and then it strikes me again.

Rain drums on my umbrella. I wait to cross Greville Road under a sign for vodka that was a sign for cider when I left. I try to see what else has changed, which is impossible. Once the road crosses into Kilburn it is shingled with posters, hoardings, flyers. London's visual tax on the poor. I pass the first of the four Carphone Warehouses on my walk home from the tube.

Inside my flat, I remove my coat, fold my umbrella. The flat seems uncanny. There is a coffee mug in the sink, rinsed but not washed, from before I went to work on Friday morning.

I walk to the window at the end of the living room and watch vapor spinning from the roofs. On clear days I can see south as far as Brixton, and east to the City. At dusk, the towers start to shimmer and haze, and by nightfall I can see a million windows.

Now, the falling rain blurs away the view somewhere around Bayswater. The white cornice roofs of houses fade under the mist, then disappear. We could have people there, said Moretti. Light a fire, make sure the boiler is on.

Rain spatters on the window. I start to move through the flat, but I can't believe I'm here. I don't know how to survive the hours until I can sleep.

I used to love coming home, fixing coffee or tea, shucking off my shoes and tights, rubbing at the red welts they left on my stomach and the ribbed lines from my socks. Now my movements are stiff as I change into a pair of leggings and a long-sleeved shirt from a race in Wandsworth that I didn't run.

I was only gone for nine days. Most of the food in my fridge is still good. I take the rubbish to the chute in the corridor. In the shower I am transfixed by the smell of my shampoo, which after nine days away seems to belong to the distant past. The steam pools the scent of rosemary and juniper around me. I'll have to buy a new kind.

When I come out of the shower, the rain has stopped and I dress and step onto the balcony, the wind in my face and whistling off the side of the building, the seagulls screaming and diving. Blood rises up my legs and the vertigo makes my head light. The fog has cleared and past the roofs of Bayswater I can see Hyde Park, which from here is a dark green stripe with silvery sheets of mist.

The air smells of paraffin. I study the skyline. The dark shape of the Lots Road power station. The Oxo Tower on the South Bank. I went to dinner there once. The restaurant at its top, the sound of the bartender pouring ice in a glass carrying across the room. Elderflower gin and tonics, I'd just met Liam and thought, I didn't know things could be like this.

My legs shake. I am scared of heights but less than I am of other things. Last spring, I entered a lift with a stranger, and after we rose past the first few floors a surge of fear crashed over me, and I was sure that he wanted to hurt me. The man stared at the join in the doors. His arms hung at his sides and his fingers curled and uncurled.

I think both of us could have recovered from the shock of her assault, if we hadn't spent months afterward learning about hundreds of other assaults and rapes and murders as part of our search for him. I wanted both of us to forget what we had learned. For the past five years, I've pretended that we did forget, and ignored any signs otherwise. That she got a German shepherd. That I never ride alone in a cab.

I don't know if I was right about the stranger in the lift. We stopped on the eighth floor and another man came inside, so he couldn't do anything even if he'd wanted to. When I told Rachel about it, arriving at her house to find her chopping coriander, a glowing blue sky over Oxfordshire, she said, "You have an overactive imagination."

"Or I picked up on something," I said, splashing white wine into a glass, remembering the man's dangling arms, his curling fingers. I must have sounded like I wanted to be right, and she frowned at me.

Rachel knew I blamed myself for what happened to her in Snaith, and that I wanted things to be even. Whatever that meant. I wished I hadn't told her. She pushed the pile of coriander against the knife blade and continued chopping.

The smell of paraffin still hangs in the air. One of the balconies below mine must be open to the flat and I can hear their music. Four on the floor. Patterns ripple across the muddy sky. I wonder if he is out there somewhere, celebrating. Rage lights through me and then, in a sea change, all my fury turns to Rachel.

I picture her leaning against the balcony with the skyline behind her. Her black jumper falls off her shoulder, showing the yellow strap of her bra. She starts to smile, her cheekbones lifting, eyes shining. If Keith watched her from the ridge, she probably encouraged him. She probably liked the attention.

The wind flattens my shirt to my chest. I cross my arms and start to go through our old fights. After the sodden misery of the past nine days, it is a joy to be spiteful, like I am swigging battery acid.

I build my case against her, based on every time she was thoughtless or nasty, like the time she called me lazy. "I'm just as ambitious as you are," I said.

"For what?" she asked. "Toward what?"

She laughed, and I said, "Well, what about you? Do you think anyone will remember you when you're dead? You're a nurse, no one thinks about you twice after they leave hospital."

"They do, and I don't care," said Rachel, with the air of a tennis player who serves a beautiful shot and throws her racket down in the same gesture.

The temper on her. She is the only woman I know to have been hit by a male bouncer. On another night, I watched her pick up two bottles of beer, hold them over the bar, and drop them on the bartender's feet.

At a party a few years ago on the island in Hackney Wick, I turned to her and said, "This is the best party I've ever been to." I resumed dancing and wondering if this was what Burning Man was like, and Rachel punched a man in the head and had us kicked out.

Alice said we needed to make her run laps before she could go out. We were at the dog park in Willesden and she pointed and said, "That's what the bitch needs." We knew the source of her fury, but it didn't always make us sympathetic.

The thought of the party on the island in Hackney Wick fills me with bitterness. I wrench open my closet and throw my bag inside. Her flannel dressing gown is on the floor. I carry the gown to the sofa and hold it on my lap. I run the fabric through my fingers. It still holds her smell, and I sink back, exhausted.

I can't wait here during the inquiry. If it was a random attack, the police will never find him. Unless he confesses. Unless a woman in the countryside outside Oxford calls and says, I doubt it's anything, but my husband came home late, and I noticed there was blood on his jacket and in his car. Do you think you should come have a look?

I clean my flat for the potential subletter. I lock the door and take a bus to Earl's Court to drop my key in Martha's postbox. The lights in her house are out, which is good. I don't want her to see me and try to convince me to stay. By eleven I am at Paddington again, waiting for the train that will take me back.

PART TWO

MARLOW

⇒ 22 ⇐

Once I followed a woman home from the tube. She got on at Monument, which in itself caught my attention. I wanted to know what she had been doing there, for some reason. She spent the trip reading, and only looked up once, at Cannon Street. When she stood at Victoria, I followed her off the train instead of staying until my stop. She left the station and walked toward the river and Pimlico. It was late May, the kind of warm spring evening when you delay going indoors. She stepped onto the road to get around the crowd of people standing outside a pub, holding sparkling glasses of lager and smoking, then turned on a small road of terraced yellow-brick houses with white piping on the roofs.

I never told anyone. It would be too hard to explain what I had wanted to know about her.

The woman in Pimlico noticed me, but she didn't think anything of it. I could have followed her up to the house, and said I lived in the flat below hers, and she would have held the door open for me and laughed at the coincidence. This is different, of course. I want Keith to notice me following him. The important thing, though, that I learned is that I appear harmless. What this means is that I can stalk him and no one will notice but him. If I walk by his house twice in one day, if we eat dinner at the same pub. I've never threatened him, he has no evidence of harassment. All I have to do, I think, is be where he is.

Keith is hiding something. Still, he might not have killed her. He might have only stalked her. And he certainly didn't assault her in Snaith fifteen years ago. I might be looking for three different men. The man who attacked her in Snaith, the man who watched her from the ridge, and the man who murdered her.

Rachel visited Bristol Prison in March, only a few months ago. She never stopped looking for the man who assaulted her. There is a chance that she found him, and he killed her. I know how she conducted her search from fifteen years ago, and whatever she found will still be available.

I leave the Hunters and go to the newsagent's for supplies. When we were teenagers, we spent hours at a time looking for him in crime reports, reading about incidents near Snaith, chewing bags of Swedish fish. Biting them off between my teeth, clicking from one rape story to the next. The smell of them turns my stomach now.

Instead I buy bags of licorice and a bottle of mineral water. I sit with my laptop on my bed, the open bags of sweets scattered around me, and begin to search for the man who attacked her.

Grievous bodily harm, rape, murder. A rough

circle with Snaith at its center, encompassing Leeds, York, and Hull, and the villages between them. As I start to read, the adrenaline takes hold. I remember this. Both of our mouths stained red, our backs hunched, legs folded under us.

Reporting has changed in fifteen years. There is more material now, more photographs. I move quickly through the stories, carried by something close to panic. It's so familiar. I thought I had changed, but maybe the years in London were the aberration, and I was always going to return to this.

By the end of the day, there is sweat pooled under my arms, and I have a list of names. The first one is Lee Barton, and in two days he will appear at York Crown Court.

➢ 23 ◅

"Is that what you're wearing?"

"Yes." Rachel wore shorts and a low-cut black tank top that showed her cleavage. We started for the bus stop. The heat wave still hadn't broken since the night of the attack. The houses on our estate looked slumped, like melting iced cakes. They would all collapse, sooner or later, and the heat seemed to be speeding them on their way. Sweat dampened the straps of my rucksack. I had packed a spare jumper for Rachel, though on all our other visits she'd refused it.

I didn't know whose job it would be to tell Rachel to dress decently. The court usher, the security guards. No one was up for it, apparently.

We had already visited the courthouse in York six times. Rachel believed she wasn't the first person he had attacked and wouldn't be the last. She thought he would be caught eventually, and we came to the court to look for him.

When asked, we said we watched trials because we planned to study law at Newcastle. "Me too!" said a boy our age once. Rachel stared at the floor and I turned to him. He wore a cheap, clean suit and a shiny tie. "At Durham, though."

He beamed at me and said, "Have you heard any interesting cases yet?"

"No," I said. "Not yet."

The guards pretended not to stare at Rachel while we went through security, until her back was to them and she lifted her arms for the female officer to pat her down. When the woman asked her to turn around, Rachel smiled at the sight of the men motionless on the queue. In the sunlight, the cotton of her top turned sheer in the triangle between her breasts, showing the skin beneath it.

As we walked down the marble corridor, I pulled on a loose jumper and put my hair back. I knew why the defendants were here and what they had done.

Today's defendant was accused of following a girl into the toilets at a pub and raping her. He said it was consensual and pled not guilty at his magistrate's hearing.

It wasn't him, Rachel knew as soon as she saw him, but neither of us considered leaving. The victim was a fifteen-year-old girl. The public gallery was empty except for us, and when the girl went onto the stand, she stared as though hoping to recognize us.

It was the second day of the trial. We didn't know what had happened on the first day, so we didn't know why she looked so desperate. The defense barrister started with a simple line of questioning about where she had been the day of the assault, and with whom. He was in his forties, with round wire glasses and a crisp accent. I was relieved for her sake that he wasn't aggressive like some of the other barristers we had seen, or the detectives who'd visited Rachel in hospital.

The girl was shaking, I thought from being in the same room as the defendant, an older teenager who ignored everyone in the room except his barrister and the judge.

The barrister gave a name and asked the girl if she knew him. She said yes, they were friends.

"Did you send photographs of yourself to him?" he asked in a level voice.

The girl hunched. "Yes."

"What was in the photographs?"

Rachel leaned forward. She wasn't looking at the barrister. She was intent on the judge. He had to stop this. The judge calmly regarded the girl, and the barrister. His face was so pale it seemed to have a layer of dust or chalk.

"I'm in them."

"What are you doing in the photographs?"

The jury appeared interested in this development. None of them frowned at the barrister. Their expressions showed only focus, an eagerness to take this new information into account.

She didn't answer.

"Are you nude in them?"

"Yes," she said.

"Why did you send the photographs?"

"I liked him."

The barrister was quiet for a long moment, as though deflated by this revelation about her. Then he straightened. "How many boyfriends have you had?" he asked, and his voice sounded confident and refreshed.

This continued for another hour. A few of the jury members finally started to appear uneasy, but most of them seemed sunk in disapproval, their minds made up about her. The judge wasn't surprised. That might have been what worried me most. He watched a middle-aged man ask a child how many times she'd had sex and if she masturbated often and if she took topless photographs, and never showed any discomfort. It must happen all the time.

The prosecutor showed photographs taken in

hospital of bruises on the girl's wrists and legs, but the jury's faces didn't turn sympathetic. The bruises didn't mean it wasn't consensual, the defense barrister argued. It might have been rough sex.

Rachel and I didn't speak as we left the court. The defendant was declared not guilty. Later we tried to find the girl, but her name had been starred out of the court records because she was a minor.

That evening we rode home in silence. The sky was still light above the shadowy trees and utility lines. The air was balmy and soft. Cow parsley grew high along the road.

"I can't do this on my own after you leave," I told her. She was moving to Manchester in September for her nursing course.

"Why not?"

"I'll be too busy. I have to study for my A levels."

She didn't look at me.

⇒ 24 ⇐

The library is one of the painted-wood buildings on the high street in Marlow. I still have Rachel's library card from the last time I borrowed it, and I need something to do at night at the Hunters. I pull out books at random. *The Lover*. *Balthazar*. *King Lear*.

Never, never, never, never, never. Kill, kill, kill, kill.

I can't remember if that is the right quote. I keep pulling books but I can't understand any of them, even the ones I have read before. The sentences don't lock together. I climb the narrow stairs to the children's collection and choose a book of German fairy tales with beautiful colored illustrations.

"You have two books overdue," says the librarian at the checkout desk. He is young, with black hair and round glasses. He doesn't live in Marlow, I've seen him waiting for the bus to Oxford with his bag on his lap.

"What are they?"

"The Nesbø and the Läckberg." He waits. Her last books. "Do you want to renew them?"

"Yes," I say, "thank you."

After the library, I drive to Abingdon. A poster in the corridor at the police station promotes an early retirement scheme, and I look between it and the book of fairy tales.

"Why don't you retire?" I ask Moretti.

"Ah," he says, "you've noticed our voluntary redundancy program." I wait. He takes off his glasses and wipes his eyelids. "It's complicated."

"You have a house in Whitstable."

"I have a shack," he says. I try to imagine him

as a fisherman, in yellow waders, steering a boat through rocks.

"We didn't find anyone at the hospital named Martin," he says. "Are you sure that's how she knew him?"

"She said he was a friend from the hospital. You didn't find anyone at all? Isn't it a common name?"

"No one in contact with Rachel, no staff or patients on her ward. What did she say exactly?"

"She said she had to hang up. She said she was going to meet a friend from the hospital named Martin."

"When was this?"

"Sunday evening."

"Where was she meeting him?"

"I don't know."

"Was she going to drive or walk to meet him?"

"She didn't tell me."

"You said before that they were going to have dinner. What made you think so?"

"Just the hour. Half six, something like that."

"The thing is," says Moretti, "we've looked at her phone and e-mail. There were no recent calls or messages to or from an unknown person, or anyone named Martin. It's likely she made a verbal agreement to meet him."

"Is that strange?"

"You know better than I do. How did Rachel normally arrange social engagements?"

"Text," I say. "And then she was always late, so

she always sent a message apologizing for being late. Is there anyone in town named Martin?"

"Yes, but he's nine years old." Moretti lifts the end of his tie and tucks it back into nothing. "Your father asked where you're staying."

"Did you tell him?"

"No."

"He's living in a hostel in Blackpool. Do you want their number?"

"No. Did you tell him Rachel owned a house?"

"Not directly, no."

He might want to move in. He might be there already, using her things, replacing her specific atmosphere with his. One of the rehabs, years ago, asked me to store his belongings. Three bin bags, which when I returned to my flat I discovered were filled with wire clothes hangers and papers and one pair of stiff, wrinkled jeans. Everything he owned.

He mostly ignored us when we were growing up. He was drinking then, though he still found jobs on building sites and kept the house in fairly decent order. Soon after we left home he lost the house, and began to drink more, and stay with friends. I don't know why it became more severe, if an event triggered it or if he was just worn down from years of managing.

We used to try to rescue him. The two of us, turning up at a house in Hull or a track in Leeds. As soon as she started working, Rachel regularly sent him money. Nothing we did helped, though, and, with shame, we stopped trying.

Moretti promises that he didn't give him Rachel's address, and we talk for another hour.

"Why did your last relationship end?" he asks.

"He was unfaithful."

"When did the relationship end?"

"In May."

It doesn't strike me as strange of him to ask. It doesn't even seem like police work. We talked about the news earlier, a political scandal in London, and I had the sense that he hadn't spoken about it with anyone yet and wanted to process it. The scandal in Whitehall certainly had nothing to do with the case. I still miss Liam. Every day I don't think of him is a triumph.

"Who was the other woman?"

"He didn't know her name. He was in Manchester for work, they met at a bar. They didn't continue to see each other."

"How did you find out?"

"I found a pair of black lace knickers in his bag. They must have gotten mixed up with his clothes when he left the hotel. I knew they weren't mine, they were a brand I'd never heard of before." The lace was the expensive kind, so delicate it's almost ragged, spidery.

→ 25 ←

I wait on a bench in the corridor of the same courthouse in York. It hasn't changed in fifteen years. Guards, solicitors, defendants, and witnesses move past me. No one asks why I am here. A transparent justice system, though the motto is in French and the judges are almost all Oxbridge. *Dieu et mon droit.* I only know what it means because I looked it up.

The court usher calls, "Lee Barton," and I find a seat in the public gallery. The only other person watching the trial is a middle-aged woman. A door opens and the jury files in, already wearing that expression, fixed, remote, as though to assure us they are worthy of the responsibility.

A bailiff enters escorting the defendant. I lean forward, with a catch in my throat. It could be the man who attacked her in Snaith. Brown eyes, narrow face. I can't gauge his height from here. He runs his eyes over the crowd, passing over me. He and the other woman in the public gallery give each other a smile. His mother, I think.

The prosecutor and the defense are both women. Both appear to be in their forties, brisk and neat. They both speak quickly, though never too quickly for the jury to understand, and with a degree of urgency. I find that I like both of them, and I wonder where they go after their trials end for the day, if they return to their offices or meet their colleagues for a drink.

I'd rather watch them, but I force myself to study Lee. He is accused of beating a woman with a tire iron. Rachel might have read about it and paid him a visit. He was released on bail until the trial and was free on the day of her murder.

The defense barrister interviews a witness, an army corporal who trained Lee. The questions are about Lee's temper, his character, and the work he did as a private and then a border guard. "What were the dates of his service?" asks the barrister.

"He served in the Yorkshire Regiment from 1996 to 1999 and as a border guard on Tortola, BVI, from 1998 to 2000."

He was abroad when Rachel was attacked. I slump against the bench and rub my hand over my eyes.

During the recess, I find the woman from the public gallery smoking outside. I ask for a light and introduce myself. "I'm Caitlin, Alex's girl-friend. He had work so he asked me to come and tell him what happened."

It always surprises me how easily the old accent comes back, as though it's been waiting, building up, growing stronger. She nods, distracted. I can't tell if the name was a success-ful guess, but if her son doesn't know an Alex, she's too preoccupied to challenge me.

"I didn't know Lee was sent to the Virgin Islands," I say. She stares across the wet traffic circle. The columns loom above us. "Did he get home much?"

"No," she says. "Only once, for Christmas."

After she returns inside, I stub out my cigarette and pass between the stained columns into the drizzle. On top of the courthouse is a statue of a blindfolded woman holding a sword and a pair of scales. The blindfold makes her look like she is about to be executed.

➤ 26 ⬅

When I return from York, the journalist is at the bar in the inn. I hurry past the open door, and there is a clatter behind me as Sarah climbs off her stool and follows me into the hall.

"Glass of wine?" she asks. I start up the stairs. "Nora, I was a court reporter at the Old Bailey for eight years. I've watched hundreds of police inquiries move to trial. I can help you."

I come down the stairs and follow her into the bar.

"This is off the record," she says. "Ask me anything you like."

"What happens to the victims' families?"

"If it's a child, the parents divorce. Even if the child is grown. The families often go into debt. It can be difficult to hold a job, especially at first. If it's a spouse, the surviving partner will often remarry, and if not, he has a high risk of an early death." She looks at me and says, "Siblings generally recover. It's not the same as losing a child."

"If there's a trial, will I be able to talk to him?"

"Sort of. You can make an impact statement, but the defendant doesn't have to respond in any way. Once he is in prison, you can visit him, if he agrees to it."

Sarah orders a glass of wine. She wears red lipstick and a loose cowl-neck sweater. In the leather satchel hanging on a hook by her legs is a scarf with a pattern of red Japanese gates, and a black notebook.

"Keith Denton was at her house that morning."

"I know. I've been looking into him," she says. "He doesn't have a record. Everyone I've spoken to here adores him."

I signal to the bartender and order a bourbon. She's telling the truth. If she'd found any dark secrets of his, they would be published by now.

"When will the police stop looking?"

"The Thames Valley CID says they keep an inquiry open until they stop turning up new evidence. But that's not true, since any information about her can be considered evidence. Really they stop when they have too many new inquiries."

"How long will that be?" There's so little crime here, I expect it could be months, a year.

"In this district, not long. Any day now."

"What?" There were only four murders in the county last year, I remember from the article about Rachel.

"They investigate murder, manslaughter, rape, missing persons, serious assault, and child abuse. They have more cases than you might think."

"Would they come back to it?"

"Yes, if there's a similar incident in the area, or if someone confesses. Or someone on the review team might pick it up, but there are hundreds of other cases for them to consider." We sit in silence, and she straightens the links on her bracelet. "Can I ask you something?" she says.

I nod, though she seems far away, and the bar seems far away. Any day now. Then I notice Sarah's expression. She's going to tell me who she thinks did it.

"Where's the dog?" she asks.

"What?"

"A lot of people in town have mentioned seeing Rachel with a dog. Where is he?"

"He ran away."

She nods and sips her wine. "When?"

"The day Rachel was killed. Whoever did it must have left the door open and the dog escaped."

German shepherds do not run away. Sarah

doesn't say this, and she tries not to look triumphant, but she is getting closer to whatever it is she needs. I can't tell you what it will be like, Moretti said, if this becomes a national story.

⇒ 27 ⇐

I take myself to the Miller's Arms for breakfast. I only pretended to Rachel that I liked the Duck and Cover better. I order the Parmesan galette and a coffee and argue with Rachel in my head. I don't want a sausage bap and instant coffee, I tell her. You're skint, she would say, that is what skint people eat.

"Social climber," she said when I was eighteen and losing my Yorkshire accent, and I was, but I also needed a change. That summer, our dad lost the plot, and by the time I got to university I was furious, and I changed my voice the way I would have chewed off my leg to get out of a trap. Every time I heard my cool, even accent, I thought—I've left, I'm gone.

It wasn't difficult. Most of the people I went to university with spoke in the almost placeless tones of Received Pronunciation. Rachel kept her accent even after she moved south, but she had a beautiful voice, burry and low.

I try not to think about my conversation with the journalist, but I regret all of what I said to

137

her. If I weighed my actions further in the past, the regret might kill me.

I told Rachel I would be on an earlier train. After my job, I was supposed to catch the 1:50 train from Paddington. Instead I left London at 2:50. In that hour, I ate lunch at the Surprise. I had salmon in pastry and a white wine. The thought of the food and drink repulses me. At the time I thought it was decadent.

Last night, I should have said one of Rachel's friends took the dog. I should have read her notebook when Sarah went to the toilet, and I should not have asked her about Keith Denton. Rachel would have done a better job of this. She would have been patient and cunning.

The owner brings me toast and marmalade, the galette, and a French press of coffee. I consider my table and the room. This is why I like the Miller's Arms better. The galette is crisp and savory. There are bright pink stalks of rhubarb on the counter. Every summer, wild rhubarb striped pink and white grows on Boar Lane. I open the book of German fairy tales.

In "The Six Swans," a girl's brothers are turned into swans for six years. If she speaks or laughs, they will remain swans forever. She sews them shirts and doesn't speak even when she is accused of murdering her children. On the last day of the sixth year, the swans fly to her. She throws the shirts on them and they turn back into men. There is an illustration of the sixth brother. The girl didn't finish his sleeve in time, so he has a swan wing in place of one arm.

Martha calls, and I talk to her outside under the yellow awning. "What are you doing? What's your routine?" she asks. Five days have passed since the funeral.

"I don't have a routine."

"But what do you do there every day? How do you spend the time?"

I consider the awning, which is translucent, glowing with sunlight. I don't want to tell her about Keith yet. "I do research. She was still looking for the man who attacked her, and I've picked up where she left off."

"Is it useful?"

"I can't tell."

"What do the police think about your staying?"

"They want me to stay in the area. We talk often."

"On the phone?" she asks, and then, without waiting for a response, she says, "How many times have they interviewed you?"

"Three or four, at the station. We've spoken a few times on the phone, but that's not an interview."

"What do you talk about?"

"The inquiry."

"You know that's not normal, don't you? You should have a family liaison officer."

"I do have one." She left me a message the day after it happened, which I never returned.

"The lead detectives don't usually keep the family updated."

"How do you know?"

"Everyone knows that. Have they interviewed you under caution?"

"No."

"Nora, do you think they're investing time in you because they like you? Either you're a suspect, or they think you know something that you're not telling them."

"I'm not a suspect. They need information about her for the victim profile." I look across the road at the black shutters on the inn. "And I want to see if anyone in town does anything strange. Having me here might make him nervous."

"If he's there," she says, "which most likely he isn't."

"Why would you say that?"

"You can't be sure that he knew her."

"He killed her dog. Why would he kill her dog unless he wanted to punish her?"

"I don't know," she says, and I can tell that she's crying and trying to pretend that she isn't. "If he were insane. That sounds like someone not in his right mind."

It's only ten thirty when I get back to my room. There are so many things to do. I should clear out

Rachel's house. I should organize her mortgage and bills. I should write notes to the people who sent flowers and wreaths to her funeral. I should earn money. I should open a new line of credit before my card reaches its limit. I should talk to a therapist or someone from Victim Support. Martha sent me a list of groups for the families of murder victims. There is one in Oxford, I should find out when it meets.

Instead I decide to go for a walk on the aqueduct. As I put on my boots, I notice a pile of white powder beside the dresser. In it are two larger pieces, and I recognize the handle and part of the base from the pitcher that used to stand on the dresser. Sometime in the night, I must have smashed it. I don't remember this at all. I don't know what I used to break it. I used to sleepwalk, the year after Rachel left home, when I was still in Snaith with our dad. I wonder what other changes are happening that I don't know about.

➜ 28 ⬳

I force myself not to walk past Keith's house. I already have twice today, before and after the aqueduct. His home isn't what I expected. I thought he would live in a house like the one where we grew up, a little plaster box built after the war, but number eleven Bray Lane is wooden, with shingles. The shingles are shaped like scallops and painted pale green. It looks like a house you'd see in a port in Denmark or Sweden.

The difficult part is going slowly. If Keith ever accuses me of following him, I have to be sure it makes him seem like the crazy one, the fixated one. All of my movements must seem natural, as though only a guilty person would notice them.

I decide to go to the grocer's in Marlow, where at least there is a chance of running into him. It's also practical. I can't afford restaurants or take-aways, and I assume I can talk the girl at the Hunters into letting me leave a few things in the restaurant fridge.

I haven't done the shopping since it happened. I remember going to the Tesco in Kilburn a few weeks ago, with all the other people who had just come up from the tube, who were also hungry and had just finished work, also buying supplies for dinner and a reward for getting through the day.

A woman lays her hand on my arm. I look down from the boxes of pasta, which I was considering, wondering if the girl at the Hunters would also let me use their hob. The woman has long, smooth hair and wears a green hunting jacket. I recognize her from walks on the aqueduct. She has two massive Newfoundlands.

I try to remember her name. Something soft and rainy and Home Counties. Was it Tamsin? I asked Rachel about her. "She looks so fresh,"

I said, "and outdoorsy." *Blooming* was the word, which I didn't intend to tell Rachel.

Rachel snorted. "Not outdoorsy," she said, "rich."

Rachel told me that she has three children and lives in the Georgian stone house that you can partly see from the aqueduct, behind a thick hedgerow.

She glances down at my basket, and I feel a stricture loosen, a sort of sigh. This is exactly what I need. She will invite me over for dinner. Maybe, eventually, she will suggest I stay with them instead of at the Hunters. I could make myself useful. Watch the children, walk the dogs. Take care of the garden, obviously. My worry over my credit debt will fade. I remember looking through the hedgerow toward her house a few weeks ago and seeing trees full of yellow apples.

"I hope they find him soon," she says. "I'm sick of being scared at night in my own house. Do you think it's someone from her Hull days?"

"Rachel never lived in Hull."

She looks at me like I am lying. "Where was it again?"

I recognize her tone. It is the voice my clients in London use when something in their garden has died or been knocked over in a storm, and they ask me to remind them of how much they paid for it.

"We grew up in Snaith."

"That's near Hull, isn't it?"

143

I tip a box of wagon wheels into my basket. "Why are you scared at night?" I ask.

"Because—"

"She died at four in the afternoon," I say. "You stupid bitch."

I step around her and carry my shopping to the till. None of you protected her, I think as I walk away from her down the aisle. It was probably one of you and the rest of you didn't see it and you let it happen.

The door to the kitchen is locked, and the girl isn't at the front desk or in her room in the attic. I search on top of all the doorways for a key. I need to put the groceries in the fridge, and then I want to cook dinner.

The carrier bags strain at my arms and I am hungry and dizzy. Finally I open the back door and set the milk and eggs and cheese on one of the flagstones. The air isn't too cold now, but it will drop to freezing in the night.

I wonder if I will still be able to use the milk after it thaws. I'm too embarrassed to return the groceries, but I don't have any money and they cost ten pounds. I stare at them and it is too much for me, these absurd worries on top of the pain, and I start to howl with my jacket bunched in my mouth.

Instead of cooking pasta in the large, dim kitchen at the Hunters and possibly beginning to feel a sliver of normalcy, I drank whisky in bed and tried to fall asleep early.

Now the Emerald Gate and the chip shop are closed, and I am thinking of what I could have eaten if I were not so stupid. Wonton soup. Moo shu pancakes with plum sauce. Scallion dumplings.

I am so tired. Right now, if the detectives called and said, "We believe this to be hopeless. We've stopped looking," I think I would be relieved.

<h1 style="text-align:center">➤ 29 ◄</h1>

In the morning, I drive to the café attached to a petrol station on the Bristol Road, a few miles outside Marlow. It looks like any other service station, but the food is delicious. I once asked Rachel why and she said, "Anders," and pointed with her fork at a man in chef's whites and a toque. I have nothing to eat at the Hunters. The milk did freeze overnight and shattered the bottle. I haven't cleaned it up yet.

Wet countryside rolls away on either side of the Bristol Road. This is where the accident Rachel told me about happened, with Callum and his girlfriend, Louise. She worked at the café, he had probably driven out to collect her.

I pass a small white cross and, soon after, pull off the road. The service station sells Esso fuel, and its icon, a red globe, towers above the empty countryside. I wonder if Louise still works here. Rachel said she looked like me.

I laugh when I see Louise. We do resemble each other. I feel a loose, happy surge of familiarity and have to stop myself from wheeling toward her. She has brown hair to her shoulders and high, wide cheekbones. She even moves like me, quick and fidgety, and she also walks with her feet slightly turned out.

As I find a table, Louise goes outside for a cigarette. She smokes with one arm crossed over her stomach and the other elbow balanced on her wrist. She looks about twenty-five. She scratches her mouth with her thumb while the smoke ladders above her.

When she sees me, I think Louise notices the resemblance too. Her eyes crinkle and her mouth slopes to the side, as though she is stopping herself from pointing it out. She wears a navy shirt and a black canvas skirt with an apron over it. "What would you like?" she asks.

"Coffee and the ebelskiver, please."

She smiles and takes the menu from me. When she sets the cup and saucer down a few minutes later, I look at her wrists and forearms in the strong light through the window. There are dark red marks on her arms, like cigarette burns, though I read once the same mark can be made with a screwdriver. Her chest and neck appear to have been lacerated or burned, leaving pale, crimped scars. One of her ears folds down. Some of the fingers on her right hand are knobby and stiff, as though they were broken once.

She doesn't have to cover the scars anymore. Everyone will assume they're from the crash.

"He beat her," said Rachel. "When they came in after the collision they were both in bad shape, but none of her injuries came from the accident. They were too old. They came from him."

That night, there are a few men inside the Duck and Cover. They must be doing a lock-in, it should have closed hours ago. The men inside the pub are laughing over the bar. One of them puts his face in his hands. Next to him, Keith shakes his head and raises a bottle to his mouth.

I settle on the bench in front of the town solicitor's, across from the pub, and unwrap the plastic from a pack of cigarettes. I cup my hands around the match while I light one. Then I take out my phone and hunch over it, smoking. I force myself not to look up for a long time, and when I do Keith is staring at me through the window.

His face is blank, his mouth sagging. I don't hold his gaze. I dial the number of my bank and hold the phone to my ear, still bowed over, still holding the lit cigarette. When I glance up again, the man next to Keith is looking at me too. He shrugs and turns back to the bar.

After another few minutes, I grind the cigarette

under my boot and walk toward the common. The yews sound like there are waves seething through them, and I wait under them in case he will follow me. Above the yews, the clock strikes in the village hall, and I walk down Salt Mill Lane toward the memorial for Callum. All the candles are lit. The shrine is beautiful and shadowy, the candles pulling deep pools of scarlet from the flowers. Candlelight flickers on my face. I read the cards again, but I don't find one from Louise.

When I return to the Hunters, the bar is unlocked, and I pull a club chair to the window facing the station.

I spent ten days here in June. The town was different then. It was like going to the beach, even though it's farther inland than London. I walked around barefoot. I bicycled on Meeting House Lane. I made a blueberry slump. Rachel worked most of the time, but when she got home from the hospital she poured us both a glass of white wine and we carried them through the field behind her house and onto the aqueduct.

I remember her laughing at something, trying not to slop the wine from her glass as she threw a stick for Fenno. Greenfinches flew between the trees. The dog raised his paw in silhouette, like a dog from the unicorn tapestries, with the embroidered woods behind him. I remember thinking that this isn't the newest moment in history but the oldest, that time isn't thinning but thickening.

It is so easy to think about her. Each memory links to another one, and time doesn't seem to pass at all. I sit for hours remembering, until the first commuters, unbearably sad, begin to arrive, waiting in the darkness on the platform for the early train to London.

⇥ 30 ⇤

I drive to the hospital to meet Joanna Cole. She and Rachel worked most of their shifts together, and Joanna may know whom she meant when Rachel said she was meeting a friend from the hospital.

The John Radcliffe is a short drive from Marlow, on the edge of Oxford. A teaching hospital, with the best surgeons and equipment. When I came to meet her once, Rachel dropped a vial in a plastic bag. She wrote something on a clipboard with a word near the top highlighted in pink.

"What's the color mean?"

"Nothing. Obfuscation."

"Really?"

"No."

I watch the door to Accident and Emergency and wait for Rachel to come out, a winter coat wrapped over her scrubs, frowning, with dark circles under her eyes and her hair scraped back from her face. She liked to sit on a certain bench, facing away from the hospital. "I spend enough time inside it," she said.

I wish I could tell her something I learned from the Thames Valley Police website, which is a rule that you have to report treasure. She would love that, like people were always finding treasure, like they would be stupid enough to report it if they did.

I try to imagine what Rachel would want to talk about if she were here. Lately she had been preoccupied with swimming. The logic seemed to be that she was so tired sleep wouldn't even help anymore, only swimming.

I can hardly bear to sit still. It's not like something that happened days ago, it's always about to happen, he's always coming up the hill.

The doors to A&E open and Joanna spots me and waves. She wears a white doctor's coat over a black suit. We've met only a few times, but Rachel often spoke about her. Joanna crosses her legs and leans against the bench. The red Casualty sign glows above the entrance.

"Have they arrested anyone yet?" she asks.

"No."

"I keep thinking about what I'd do to him if I found him," says Joanna. "It wouldn't be quick."

She's from Manchester, and her accent is familiar and reassuring, not quite like Rachel's but at least northern. She is over forty and Rachel once said she looked at Joanna to see what she would be like in ten years. "But she's a doctor, not a nurse," I said, and Rachel gave me a long stare.

"Is there anyone on staff named Martin?"

Joanna frowns. "Not in our unit, no."

"A patient?"

"No one comes to mind. Why?"

"She mentioned the name for the first time recently. She said she was going to meet him."

"I'll let you know if I think of anything," she says.

"How had she seemed lately?"

"She was herself." Joanna stares at the hospital. "It's terrible without her. Everyone else in there is a tosser or a moron."

"What about Helen?"

"Tosser."

In ten years Rachel would have been a senior nurse practitioner. I wonder if she would have stayed in Oxford or left for another hospital.

"We got pissed a few weeks ago. I told Rachel about the affair I'm having and she told me about getting beat up when she was seventeen."

"She never told anyone that. I don't think she ever told Stephen."

"We were friends," says Joanna, drawing out the last word.

"Where were you?" I want to be able to picture the two of them. It makes me happy. Sometimes I worried that Rachel was lonely, that all she did was work.

"The Pelican."

Joanna sighs. I imagine she feels as I do, which is leaden. A plane roars overhead, hidden in the seam of the clouds.

"Why did you go to the Pelican?"

After work, Rachel only ever went to the White Hart, near the hospital.

"Rachel came to meet me after her shift. I was already in Oxford," she says.

"Why?"

"A coroner's inquest."

"When was this?"

"October."

"That must have been difficult."

"No, I've been at dozens of them. We do an inquest every time someone dies within forty-eight hours of entering hospital. The coroner talks to the witnesses and presents the cause of death, and then if we're lucky we have the afternoon off."

I ask about her affair, because I want to build out the image of the two of them in the Pelican. The affair is with her son's swimming instructor. I make her tell me Rachel's reaction. Joanna says there was a lot about it the two of them found hilarious at the time, and I see Rachel, hanging her dark head and laughing over the table.

Four old men are playing shuffleboard at the public courts when I return to Marlow. When it was too cold for me, Rachel played with the regulars. She didn't know all their names and said they rarely talked, but when one of them went on holiday he brought her a small bottle of ouzo.

"Why did he get you ouzo?" I asked.

"Because he went to Greece," she said.

I wonder if one of these men brought Rachel the ouzo. They appear to be in their eighties, so I rule them out of suspicion. It's not fair, really. Who knows what they were like when they were younger.

I watch them push the burgundy disks down the court and wonder whether they knew her, and how well. I remember how embarrassed Lewis was for me on the common last week. Rachel never told me about visiting Andrew Healy in prison. She never told me she bought the dog for protection. She allowed me to pretend it was over.

➔ 31 ◆

I come out of the grocer's on the high street with two carrier bags. Part of my arrangement with the manager now is that I have full use of the kitchen. There are flurries but it feels too cold for snow. I shift the straining bags to my other hand. At the door to the inn, I turn around and, as I expected, Keith is standing beside his van watching me.

I was behind him on the checkout line. It was quite a slow line, too. He seemed to grow more and more distraught, but he couldn't exactly leave at the sight of me, at least not in front of other people. The thing is, Rachel and I look similar.

I resume my research, hunched over my laptop on the bed, working through a bag of licorice. I add more names to the list and sort through them, striking names if they were in prison on the date of either her assault or her murder, adding stars to indicate priority, and then, hours into the research, I find Paul Wheeler.

It took me so long because he was charged six years ago, and there's been nothing about him in the news since. He attacked a young woman at seven in the morning in Bramley, a district in Leeds. As soon as I read the first sentence of the article, my skin starts to burn.

Seeing the photograph of him is like remembering a name you've forgotten, as though I knew it was him all along. He looks exactly as she described.

I lurch off the bed and drink water straight from the tap. I want to call Rachel so much that I pick up my phone and find her name, allowing myself a few seconds with the illusion that I might be able to tell her.

The assault matches what happened to Rachel. The victim was a stranger, the attack brutal and sudden. After another two hours of research, I have the name of the victim, the town where Paul lived, and the name of his solicitor. He was tried at York Crown Court and imprisoned at Wakefield. I call his solicitor and leave a message with my number, asking Paul to contact me. I say my name is Sarah Collier, from the *Telegraph*. A few hours later, my phone rings.

We arranged to meet at a café in Leeds. I am surprised that he is willing to talk to me, though he has nothing to lose. He has already served time for the assault in Bramley. If his case hadn't yet gone to trial, or if he were still in prison awaiting parole, he would never agree to meet me.

His hair has been shaved. Before, in the arrest photographs, he wore it long. He hasn't seen me yet and I step back into the entry. I can't go near him when I'm like this, and I force myself to wait outside for another few minutes. He is on parole. I know the conditions of his parole and what will happen if he violates them.

He smiles when he sees me. It's him. I'm certain of it. There is a glass jar of sugar on the table, and I want to break it in half on the edge of the chair and drive it into his face.

"Hello, Paul. Thank you for meeting me." I imitate Sarah Collier. I speak in a brisk voice, as she does, and my movements are firm and decisive. After my coffee arrives, I tap my spoon once on the side of the cup and set it beside my saucer. "I'm working on a story for the *Telegraph* and it concerns you. I think there was a miscarriage of justice in your trial."

It takes a great deal of effort to speak clearly and sound neutral. If I stop controlling my face for a second, it will break apart, and I will tell him how I plan to punish him.

He stares back at me, amused, and I think the disguise hasn't convinced him, but he probably does this to all women—journalists, prosecutors, judges—a stripping-down, an assessment. Their reserve and competence don't fool him. He knows what they're like. He knows what they look and sound like when they're scared.

I let my features slip, to show him my distaste, as an actual journalist might. We stare frankly at each other for a moment, then I signal to the waiter and order a danish. It's a calculated gesture. I'm not too frightened to eat in front of him.

"Do you want anything?"

"No," he says, and I study him. Did you hurt my sister? Did you kill her? I think of the woman in Bramley. Both of her shoulders were dislocated by the time he was done.

"Have you heard of Anna Cartwright?" I ask.

"No."

"She was a forensic pathologist in the US. A few years ago, she was caught falsifying evidence. Her work was used in thousands of convictions, and all of them have to be retried now. I think something similar is happening in York."

"Who?"

"I can't say yet. But the person handled materials for your trial."

"It's too late now, isn't it?" he says. "I already served five years."

"You could clear your name. It must be difficult to find work."

"No," he says, "it hasn't been."

"The story will go ahead either way. If you want a chance to say what actually happened, all you have to do is talk to me." The waiter sets down the danish and I start to eat, choking down the sweet cream and pastry. I hate danishes, but didn't want to ruin a good food.

"How much will I be paid?"

"We don't compensate interview subjects, but you might receive reparations if your conviction is overturned." I pause, as though this next part will be difficult to hear. "He's done very well, this man. He's risen quickly in the Home Office."

We talk for the next half hour. He grew up in Hull and attended the comprehensive on Fountain Road. He lived in Hull until he was charged, and I work out that he was there the summer of Rachel's assault. He spent five years at Wakefield Prison. His brother bought him a flat and furnished it for him before his parole.

"Did your brother collect you on your release?"

"No. He lives in Germany."

I falter for a moment. His brother thinks he's guilty. He flew back to buy and furnish the flat, but not to meet him. I would guess he never visited Paul in prison either.

We discuss his treatment by the police. He has some complaints but was treated courteously overall. He mentions his probation officer by name. He tells me about being on parole and about his job.

As we finish the conversation, I mention the name of the commissioning editor at the *Telegraph*.

He smiles. "Do you live in London?" he asks.

"Yes."

"Where?"

"Clapham," I say, with a tight smile. He tilts his head. He knows I'm lying, but I think it pleases him that I don't want him to know where I live. I stow my notebook in my bag. I'm about to pull the straps over my shoulder and stand when he says, "We've met before. Do you not remember?"

"No."

"At the Cross Keys."

"I've never been. Is that around here?"

"Yes. You must have been a teenager. We talked one night. You don't remember our conversation?"

"No. I've no idea what you're talking about."

⇥ 32 ⇤

I leave the car in front of the café and walk to Albion Street. The district is familiar, though many of the shops have changed since I was last here, years ago. The name of the pub isn't familiar, and I was telling the truth when I said I'd never been to it. A group of us often went out in Leeds when we were teenagers, but I remember the names of the bars and clubs, and the Cross Keys isn't one of them. People go past me, pulling their collars up, the rain too fine for an umbrella. I turn into Red Lion Square.

The pub has an ordinary front—baskets of ivy, a chalkboard by the door—but as soon as I see it I know that the bar is on the left when you enter and there is a square stone patio for smoking. The toilets are down a flight of stairs behind red stall doors that are half the usual height.

The pub has a few patrons inside, stale air, a race on. I go down the steps, and at the bottom of the stairs I push open the door to the ladies'. I still hope to be wrong. The room smells of disinfectant and spilled liquor. The stall doors are red and half height.

I enter one of the stalls and pull the latch across. The glossy red paint shows my reflection, a dark smear. My heart is beating so strongly that when

I look down it's lifting the fabric of my shirt.

At the top of the steps the bartender and the other drinkers turn to look at me, and I realize I'm panting. It was like being where something terrible had happened, where someone had died or where bodies were buried. I don't know what happened there.

I leave the square and realize the pub is a few blocks from the Mint. We often went into places like it to drink before we went to a club. No one noticed if we brought a plastic bottle of tequila and emptied it into a cup of ice. I think Rachel and I came together. Going out in Leeds was an endeavor and something we rarely did separately.

He may have confused me with Rachel. He may have spoken to Rachel before the attack, on one of the nights when she blacked out. Or he spoke to me, on one of the nights I blacked out.

Paul told me he works as a clerk at a computer repair shop. I call the manager and introduce myself as Ruth Foley, Paul's parole officer, and ask to confirm his account of his movements. I ask if he worked on Friday 19 November, and the manager has me hold the line, then says, "Yes, he was here from ten until six."

The manager promises that he couldn't have left. He was behind a till and would have needed a replacement.

I call Moretti from the green on Merrion Street.

"What will you do if you find the man who attacked her in Snaith?"

"We would consider him as a suspect in her murder."

"What if he has an alibi? Would you investigate the assault itself?"

"No."

"Why not? There's no statute of limitations on it."

"The victim can't testify, and there were no witnesses. Even if we charged him, the Crown prosecutor would never bring it to court."

On the drive home, I think about the red half-height doors. They were designed, I think, to keep you from doing things you shouldn't. I have a memory of laughing about this. I think I went into one of the stalls with a man.

⇒ 33 ⇐

When I return to Marlow, I go to the library. On the landing, there is a drawing of the meeting house, a white lodge on a great lawn. It had a portico with columns and segments of shade, and benches facing the village. I wonder if anyone died when it burned down.

"Why didn't they rebuild it?" I asked Rachel.

"They all left. They moved to America."

I climb the stairs to the children's collection. I choose a book of Italian fairy tales with a green cover and carry it home. As I come up the stairs, I stub my toe on the chair on the landing. Pain bursts up my calf, and I drop the book. I lift the chair and thrash it against the wall. Across the landing the heavy gold mirror rattles. Dust rises from the plaster. My face is wet and my mouth gapes open as I grunt with the effort.

When I leave my room again, the book of Italian fairy tales has been smoothed and left in front of my door. On the landing, I kneel and brush the plaster dust into my hand. The exterior walls of the Hunters are made of stone. There is a chance no one will notice the dents in the plaster. Someone has already cleared away the broken chair.

That night, in my room, I try to read the Italian stories, but even they are beyond me. For a long time I sit with the book on my lap and my head tilted back in pain. When I finally stand to go to bed, I notice the illustration that has been open on my lap.

There are two rows of pleached hornbeams on a lawn that leads to a forest. A woman in a hooded robe walks purposefully toward the woods, between the hornbeams. A greyhound trots ahead of her.

My head droops toward the painting. It bewilders me, after today. I can't believe such things exist, both the painting and the things in it. The greyhound and the hooded robe. I want to know where the woman is going, and I want to be in her place with an urgency that surprises me, and that I would have thought I had outgrown.

My hands are still white with plaster dust. There are still black spots on the wall from the bottle of wine that exploded the night before her funeral.

⇥ 34 ⇤

Rachel and I visited the Tate last year. I like Tate Modern better. At its bar you can drink a white wine or a mineral water and look down at the cloudy river and St. Paul's and the people on the bridges. I didn't try to explain this to Rachel. She would fixate on the mineral water, which I rarely bought and always with a sense of disappointment in myself.

The mineral water fits, I wanted to tell her. It fits there.

We looked at medieval Flemish paintings. One of them was a triptych of a pilgrimage, and the path curved far back into the picture field. Looking at it is supposed to be like going on a pilgrimage yourself, said the placard, which I thought was overstating the matter. But it was mesmerizing, and I did find that I really wanted to be there, not here. Walking past, apparently, all manner of things. A hydra in the courtyard of an inn. Dogs chasing a leaping stag. A tavern on stilts in a pond.

Rachel came over and I leaned against her and said, "Wouldn't that be nice?"

"Mm."

I followed her into the next room, where there was an oil painting of Judith and Holofernes. Holofernes was the general of an invading army. Judith seduced him and maneuvered her way into his tent. She slaked him with wine and cut off his head.

"Then what happened?" I asked, but the placard didn't say and Rachel was already in the next room.

⇥ 35 ⇤

The next day, there are cars parked in double rows along the common, and all the shops on the high street are closed. The Duck and Cover is closed, and the Miller's Arms. The only open office belongs to the town solicitor, who tells me that today is Callum Hold's funeral.

I don't have anything else to do, so I find a bench on the common. From here, there is no sign of the two hundred people inside the church. Its wooden doors are closed. Every so often a twist of smoke rises from its chimney. The garden beside it, with thin stone tablets under the cedar elm, is quiet. The church looks cold and empty, the stained glass black and glossy as oil.

Above me the yews creak in the wind. The town didn't shut down for Rachel. Or maybe the shops did close. I wouldn't have noticed. The day is bleak, and I stuff my hands in my pockets and pull my scarf over my mouth.

I think about the Cross Keys and the red half-height doors in the toilets. I still can't remember what happened there. Every time I think of it, my stomach drops, as it does when I remember something shameful.

With a sound like a gate being lowered, the church doors open. The family appears to be the first to come out. They're down from Stoke, said the town solicitor. There isn't a coffin.

Callum died in September. The solicitor told me the family waited to have the funeral until his best friend returned from a tour in Afghanistan. I can't tell who he is. The best man, in a way. There are a lot of men around Callum's age, and they all look gutted.

More and more people exit the church. They spill onto the common, near where I sit. I unwind my red scarf and stuff it in my pocket since it marks me out too much. I listen to the voices, which are low and somber. Some of the men and women are still crying freely. People form groups near the open doors of the church, on its lawn, in the middle of the road along the common. I don't see Louise. I wouldn't go either, if I were her.

The reception is in Brightwell. Someone has rented the manor lodge. I know the building, which is long and low, with three turrets. When they host weddings, they fly white pennants from the turrets. I wonder if there will be flags today, and what color they will be.

When I go out again later the shops and pubs are still closed, their owners out in Brightwell. I imagine the young men I saw outside the church standing on the lawn in front of the lodge and smoking.

➤ 36 ◆

Keith has gained weight. He looks like a different man from the one who approached me on the aqueduct.

We are drawing closer. Today, he did leave a checkout line when I stood behind him. He put a full basket of food down and fled. People noticed, and after he had gone a number of them stared at me, as though they wanted to ask me what had just happened and what it meant.

Early in the evening, I run into Lewis on Meeting House Lane. "Want to go for a walk?" he says. "I could use a break."

I nod, though it's not really a break for him, anytime he talks to me he is working. I wonder what he thinks he might still discover. His legs are longer than mine, but he walks slowly, like we're only out for a stroll.

"Where are you from?" I ask.

"Brixton."

"I like Brixton."

"All of you like Brixton," he says.

"Fuck off," I say, but he's smiling, and I remember that he knows about how we grew up. I can't tell him about Paul Wheeler, not until I've decided what to do. I wish I could stop seeing his face.

"Where in Brixton?"

"Loughborough."

"I can see Loughborough from my flat."

"How did you know what it was?"

"I wanted to know what I was looking at."

We walk past the rill, which is frozen now. You could walk on it instead of on the planks laid across it.

"Why did you become a policeman?"

"For a day job," he says. "I was a musician. You have a lot of time on your own as a constable. A lot of time walking. I spent it composing songs."

"Were you in Brixton?"

"No, Barnes, where nothing ever happened," he says.

"What's your first name?"

"Winston."

"If I look you up, will I find any of your music?"

"No," he says, "definitely not."

I wonder what confidences he expects in exchange for this, but I don't have any. I wish I did. We both know he shouldn't have told me that, he should have said he wanted to help people.

"Do you miss London?" I ask.

"Yes. Do you?"

"I don't know." We start down the high street. "I was jealous of Rachel for living here. I hate London sometimes."

"Centuries of people," says Lewis, his low voice cresting up and down, "have hated London."

The town is quiet. A few people are running errands. Coming calmly out of shops, unlocking their cars or walking down the pavements. Behind us is the rosy light in the church tower.

"Do you?" I ask.

"No," he says. We walk past the bakery, and the queue inside it for bread and cakes. "I hate this." We walk past the wine shop and the building society. "No grit. No culture. It's boring."

We reach the train station and return to the common on the north side of the road.

"It's placid."

"Exactly," he says.

We walk past the chip shop. I stare in its window and then down the road, astonished. "It's like

Snaith," I say. "It's like the town where we grew up."

"We always repeat our mistakes," says Lewis.

"I never realized before. It's like Snaith but farther south."

"And with money," says Lewis, and I nod. The only difference is that time has been kind to this town and not to Snaith.

"Why did she move here?" I ask.

Lewis doesn't answer. He already has, in a way. "What do you hate about London?" he asks.

"The noise."

"The noise is the best part," he says.

We walk past the Miller's Arms. In this light its awning is the color of paper.

"Not in Kilburn."

"You can wear headphones. Do you know what you can't do anything about? The rain," he says, so the word turns long and threatening.

After Lewis returns to the station, I walk through the village again. I miss Snaith. The Vikings and the bakery. The Norman church, especially in winter, with snow falling over it and the poplars in its yard.

I can't believe I never noticed before. I walk around the common but I see the common in Snaith. The towns are like twins.

I walk past the Chinese restaurant where Lewis and I ate two weeks ago. There was one in Snaith too, though it was called, embarrassingly, Oriental Chop Suey, and this one is the Emerald Gate.

I don't know anyone else who moved to a small town. Rachel said she wanted to be close to the hospital, but Oxford would have been closer. It's as if she never left our village. I stand on the station platform and see the station in Snaith. I don't know if they have updated the trains on the Leeds line. When we lived there the seats were made of blue carpet and you could open the windows.

⇒ 37 ⇐

I bicycle down the Bristol Road, past the white cross marking the site of Callum's accident, toward the service station. Ahead of me, the red Esso globe rises above the flat countryside.

Louise is still working at the café. She wears the same clothes as last time, a navy shirt and black canvas skirt under an apron. "Hello again," she says. "Is that your bike?"

"Sort of." I don't think anyone will miss it. I found it in the shed behind the inn. Its gears are rusted and both its tires needed air.

"Do you want to bring it around back so it doesn't get wet?"

The rain has stopped but the clouds are low and ragged. Louise leads me outside and I wheel the bike around the building to a covered parking bay. You can't see the white cross from here, which is probably good. Rachel showed it to me a few weeks ago. We were on our way to Didcot, and she pointed and said, "That's where Callum's car spun off." I remember thinking it was strange, since there weren't any turns or obstacles. It was a straightaway. He must have thought he saw something in the road, a fox maybe.

The lorry bay smells of stone. I lower the kickstand and follow Louise around the building. Cars rumble down the Bristol Road. "Thanks," I say.

"Not a problem," she says.

"He beat her," said Rachel.

Louise swings open the door and holds it for me. I pass so close I can smell that she wears scent with some vetiver in it.

"How did you know her injuries came from him?"

"She told me," said Rachel.

Louise finds a breakfast menu and follows me to a table.

"Do you live around here?"

"Kidlington," she says. I wait for her to add more. I expect she is moving soon. I watch her cross the restaurant and picture a room with a friend in Camden. For some reason my image is about forty years out of date. They have a gas ring and a record player, and they go to the trattoria on the corner for a liter of red wine and bucatini.

You should move to Camden, I want to tell her. You should move to Camden in about 1973.

I wish we could talk. I want to ask her about Callum, and the accident. I can't see a way to do this without bringing Rachel into it, though I wouldn't mind that. I'd like to know what their encounter was like. But it would also mean revealing a violation of patient rights. Rachel should never have told me about Louise's injuries, or how she got them.

I finish the ebelskiver, a sort of pancake filled with jam, and pay the bill.

"Do you want to wait it out?" asks Louise. Heavy rain falls on the countryside, and we both watch as the wind blows an opaque curve of water across the road.

"It's not far. I'm staying at the Hunters in Marlow."

"Still," she says, but she doesn't ask what I am doing in Marlow. I don't think she knows I'm Rachel's sister.

I want to tell her about the moment between opening the door of the house and understanding what had happened, when what I felt was wonder. It was an incredible feeling, golden and drugged. I would like to know if she experienced that, when the car first jerked, maybe. I wouldn't mind living my whole life in that gap, when I knew the rules had somehow been upturned, but not how.

I pedal down the Bristol Road. I don't think I will see Louise again. I want to ask her why she hasn't quit already. She must find it difficult to drive past the accident site twice a day. Maybe she forces herself, as a reminder of something.

In Marlow, people have started hanging wreaths on their doors. Square and round wreaths of bay leaves and holly.

There are trees for sale at the repair garage. Last year Rachel took the tree down on Twelfth Night. "You don't want to anger the Holly Man," she said.

A bouquet of white roses has been propped in front of my door. I bend down and carry them into my room, and the soft, creamy petals fill the air with scent. I've never been given white roses before, or bought them for myself, and in the dim room they look rare and precious. I fill a glass with water for them. Someone sending condolences. Martha's family, maybe. The card is from a florist's shop in Oxford.

It says, *Nice to meet you again. Paul.*

I sit on my heels in bed holding the carving knife. My body is stiff with fear. The manager sleeps in a set of rooms on the floor below mine, and I don't know if sounds can reach her from here. It's only the pipes, the building settling. It's nothing, I imagine Rachel saying to herself on Friday, there's no one there.

⇢ 38 ⇠

Moretti calls the next morning to say that officers will be returning to her house to conduct another search of the property. He won't tell me why exactly, but I assume for the murder weapon. They still haven't found the knife.

"Are you sure Stephen was in Dorset that day?"

"Why? Did Rachel ever say she was frightened of him?"

"No."

"Was he ever violent toward her?"

"No."

"Stephen was at work until seven on the day of the murder. He placed calls from the restaurant, and he's on the security film."

"After her funeral, he said if she'd married him she would still be alive."

"And you think he was confessing?"

"No. It just seems like a strange thing to say."

I struggle not to tell him about the roses. The card was written in cursive, as though dictated, and the florist's shop confirmed that he placed the order and a courier delivered them. But he still knows where I am, and to find me in Marlow, he had to know Rachel's name. Mine doesn't appear in any of the articles about her. I think he assumed I would be at the Hunters because it's the only inn in town, though he may have learned some other way. Maybe he followed me.

I can't ask Moretti for advice. Instead, I say, "Do you have brothers or sisters?"

"One brother."

"Are you close?"

"No." He probably makes the trip to Glasgow out of duty exactly once a year, and hates every moment of it. He must be able to use his work to get out of family occasions. I can so clearly see him taking a phone call, in a house in Dalmarnock or Royston, and saying, "Sorry, I've got to go." His family must know better than to ask. It could be important.

"Have you ever been to the Whistlestop in Paddington station?" he asks.

"Yes."

"Have you made any purchases?"

"I bought wine on my way to Rachel's sometimes. Why?"

"Just a loose end," he says.

⇥ 39 ⇤

Rachel said there was something wrong with the town. I still don't know what she meant. I've hardly left its center, and today I walk north away from the lanes and the high street toward the tennis court, a strange empty box in the pines. The gate is padlocked, and cracks splinter across the court. There are still names from last season on the clipboard hanging from the fence. I walk closer. The paper has turned stiff and crinkled, and the black ink is now burnt umber. I run my finger down the page until I land on her handwriting, then stumble away from the fence.

We played tennis in August. Rachel wrote our names and we waited for the court to be free. We watched other people play, and the balls arcing back and forth over the net. The court is set in chalk, surrounded by scrub pines. I felt like we were at the beach. A turquoise sky arched above the court and the pines had squiggly tips, like cypresses.

I hurry away. The track curves so when I turn around again the court is hidden. No one has driven here recently. Weeds have sprouted from the road, and down its center they form a hedge of thistle, campion, bloody cranesbill.

Rachel borrowed the rackets, I remember. She went to get them while I waited by the Hunters. It was hot and the white canvas umbrellas were open alongside the inn.

"Where did you get those?" I asked.

"Keith," she said. I didn't ask who that was. My stomach turns, and I can't believe I didn't remember until now.

She went down the high street and came back with two rackets. I sat at one of the wooden tables outside the inn and waited for her.

He told me he barely knew her. By the time I reach the common, it's raining. I can see one of the twins inside the hardware shop. I turn down Bray Lane and stop in front of the shingled house. I wonder if Rachel ever went inside it.

His van is in the drive, but the house is dark. There is a fireman's decal in an upstairs window, in one of the children's rooms. I wait, but I don't want to talk to him in front of them or his wife.

I can't remember what Rachel said about returning the rackets. I don't remember her returning them that day, which would imply she was going to see him later. I have no idea. I remember what we ate that afternoon. Runny cheese and bread and swing-top bottles of dandelion and burdock.

This was the sort of thing she hated me for.

The Duck and Cover is full for the Arsenal and Chelsea match, and I push through the crowd until I find Keith. "Can I speak to you outside? It won't take a minute."

His eyes are glassy. He wants to tell me to fuck off, but people around us are listening, and he follows me outside. The painted-wood buildings creak in the wind, and the hanging sign of the pub rocks back and forth.

"She borrowed tennis rackets from you," I say.

"Did she?" He wears the same long coat as before and a rolled orange hat.

"This past summer."

"I never knew if she ended up using them. I left them out by the back door for her."

"Why?"

"She said she wanted to play and I said she could borrow them anytime."

"Where? Where were you when she said that?"

"Her house. She wanted an estimate on external piping."

"What for?"

"An outdoor shower," he says. "She said it was a birthday present for you."

I laugh. The dark street seems to slip and keel.

"She needed rackets, and I told her we always have that sort of thing lying around."

The rackets were new. I remember the smell of them and the tacky rectangle where a label had recently been scraped away.

⇒ 40 ⇐

I pulled last night. There was a man alone at the bar at the Mitre in Oxford, and I chose him. As a precaution, I told myself, to distract me from doing something stupid. We drank gin and tonics and talked at the bar, and I remembered how to turn the lights on, how to dispense the right amount of warmth and cruelty. On the bar were silver bowls filled with ice and bottles of cava with horned yellow labels. He was handsome, and the encounter was surreal, and jolly, as they can be sometimes, as though we had a snow day when everyone else had work. He was in town from London for a wedding, the first of his friends to arrive. They had rented a house for the weekend near Somerville College. We fucked on the stairs and in the bedroom. Because I'd had enough to drink and because the sex went on for long enough, I was able to lose where I was.

In the morning, he said, "Do you want to come to the wedding tomorrow night?"

I laughed, and he said, "No, I'm serious."

"I have work," I said.

⇒ 41 ⇐

At the holiday market on the common, the residents of Marlow tread muddy paths in the snow. Above the yews, the sky is gray. The stalls are all open, their Dutch doors flung wide. I move down the row. Soap and candles, mostly. A banner on the village hall announces the holiday fundraiser.

"What are they raising money for?" I ask a woman selling cups of pear cider.

"The bridge."

"What's wrong with the bridge?"

"It's falling down."

People can't possibly use as many soaps and candles as they buy, yet here they are, buying soaps and candles. At least there are food stalls. The first one sells pies. The second sells preserves and clary wine from a farm in Cirencester.

The next stall sells taper candles made by nuns in France, and I imagine a nun dipping the wick into a cauldron of hot wax. How do the monastic orders decide what to make or train? Saint-Émilion, Chartreuse, Saint Bernards. At the monastery in Valais, the dogs are trained to perform rescues in pairs. I am thinking of the Saint Bernards, and trying to do this without also thinking of Fenno, when a woman pats my arm.

"Rachel was truly a beauty," she says, and then she looks at me to see how I will take it. I sigh. I was jealous of her, but not for the reason everyone assumes. The woman is still watching me with that look, curious and a little mean, familiar to every sister of an exceptionally appealing woman. I can't think what to say. The yew branches lift and stream in the wind.

"She'd rather be alive."

The woman looks at me with disapproval, like I've cheated at a game. I move away from her and the taper candles.

The priest has propped open the church doors,

hopefully, in case the crowd might spill over. It must be very cold inside.

I buy a paper cup of glügg. This is why people move to small towns, I think. To gossip and raise money for the bridge.

Across the common, Keith Denton speaks with a small boy. From their interaction, I think the boy is his son and that he is a good father, loving and lighthearted. The boy runs to join the pack of children playing behind the stalls, and Keith puts his arm around a woman. He looks across the common, and when he faces in my direction, he pretends not to see me and turns so the woman under his arm rotates away.

My stomach hollows. I keep watching but Keith doesn't look over again. After a while, his wife kisses him on the cheek and slips out from under his arm to join two other women. She doesn't know about me, he hasn't confided in her. Keith stays to talk with the owner of the hardware shop, then he walks over to say something to his wife and leaves. I watch him walk down the high street until the bend in the road.

I go in the opposite direction, onto Redgate. Keith was at her house that day. He doesn't have an alibi. He offered to help me with the arrangements. He bought the tennis rackets for us to use. Rachel said she would never have an affair with a married man, which means that if she did, she wouldn't tell me. I don't think she would tell Helen either, since her husband slept with someone else when she was pregnant with Daisy, but I call her anyway.

"Was Rachel seeing anyone recently?"

"She saw Stephen sometimes."

"Anyone else?"

"I don't know," she says. I walk past the yard with the apple tree. A dozen apples singed red by the cold still hang from the bare branches.

"Did she ever talk about someone in town?" I ask.

"No."

"What about someone who was married?"

"No, she didn't."

I stand at the end of Redgate, sour with disappointment, but then Helen says, "I'm glad you called." I look across the road to the repair garage and wonder if this is it, if she has realized she knows what happened. She says, "Did you tell Daisy to go to Rachel's house?"

I wince. At the Miller's Arms, after the funeral, I remember telling Daisy to choose something from the house.

"Do you know what that place looked like? Nobody had cleaned it yet. She hasn't slept in a week. She's been doing research on sex crimes."

"Why does she think it was a sex crime?" I ask, and Helen shrieks. I turn the phone away and look at the line of poplars next to the repair garage.

"If you talk to my daughter again, I'll tell the police you've molested her."

I laugh. She hangs up and I stare at the phone, shaking.

"Why did you interview Keith Denton?"

"The plumber?" says Moretti. "Why?"

I wait.

"He was the last known person to see her alive," he says.

"Did they have a relationship?"

"Not one that I know about. Do you have something to tell me, Nora?"

"No."

The police interviewed him three weeks ago, and Moretti told me then that they were testing his van and house for forensic evidence. I remember the fireman's decal in the window and wonder where his wife took their children while the police searched the house.

"What's his wife's name?"

There is silence on the line. I knew he would be reluctant to tell me, but there's no reason for him to refuse. It's a small town, I'll be able to find it.

"Please, Rachel might have mentioned her."

"Natasha," he says.

I am standing by the rill when Keith comes off the high street. We're alone, though I can hear sounds from the holiday market. I finger the straight razor I've started to carry, the sort of blade that before I only ever saw when a clerk used it to scrape the sticker from a bottle of wine.

"I'm keeping a log," Keith says, "of every time you walk past my house and every time you follow me inside somewhere."

"That seems odd," I say. "It makes sense we'd run into each other in a small town."

He has gained more weight. I would eat a lot too, if I were faced with a lifetime of prison food.

"You'll be caught," he says.

"For what?"

"Stalking."

"No, I don't think so." I turn away from him, toward the rill, and consider it with my hands in my pockets. I use the toe of my boot to brush the snow on its surface, then turn back toward him. "Do you think your wife knows what you've done?"

He slaps me. It lands hard and my skull rattles. My head starts to pound, but it won't leave much of a mark. He checks that no one saw and strides back to the high street.

I soon find a Natasha Denton who works at a spa with locations in Bath and Oxford. When I call the North Oxford branch, the receptionist tells me that Natasha does work on Sundays, but her appointments for tomorrow are all booked, starting at nine in the morning.

⤜ 42 ⤛

"I need to ask you something."

I don't know what to say next. I've never had to doorstop someone's wife before. Thanks, Rachel.

I've been waiting for her in the car park outside the spa for the past hour. She looks at me, puzzled, trying to work out if I am a client or someone with a habit. "Can we go somewhere?"

Her face starts to morph. It sags and grows soft with fear. "No," she says. "I've got to go to work."

"It's about your husband."

It seems pointless to say. She already knows it is. Natasha sneers and steps back. She looks at me and I can see her thinking, No accounting for taste.

"I think he had an affair with my sister."

"Who?"

"Rachel Lawrence."

Relief slips over her face, and she lowers her eyes. "No, you're wrong. He already talked to the police."

"I'm asking you. If there's anything you noticed, if he has ever acted strange, about going somewhere or meeting someone."

"He hasn't."

"Then when you saw me—just now—why did you think I'd been having it off with him?"

"I didn't," she says and laughs. "I thought you were going to rob me."

I don't believe her, but, then, I also can't remember the last time I showered, or put anything on the dark, shiny smudges under my eyes.

"My sister killed herself on her twentieth birthday," she says. "If I could help you, I would, I promise."

"Does he have a middle name?"

"Yes," she says and clears her throat. She looks nervous. "Thomas."

Martha answers from her dressing room at the Royal Court.

"What happens when you have an affair?" I ask.

"You get fit," she says. "You spend money on different things. You start to spend time in other parts of the city."

Martha has complained to me before that half of the plays running in London at any given time revolve around an affair. She has played an adulterer or mistress in a dozen productions. She last acted in *Betrayal*, in which the lovers buy a flat in Kilburn. I can't imagine Rachel doing that. It seems outdated, buying a flat for adultery, like owning a gas ring, and financially impossible. Normal people couldn't do that anymore, you couldn't shift enough money to buy an entire flat.

"Is there anything else?"

"Something to do with your phone. You might get a second one, or start spending more time on it," she says. "How are you?"

"Fine. I have a routine now," I say, though that's not quite right, it's less of a routine than a reason.

"Come home," says Martha. "I made a copy of my keys for you."

"I can't."

"She isn't watching, Nora. You can't make it up to her."

"What about presents? Isn't that something people do in an affair?"

I'm meeting a friend named Martin, said Rachel, on the Sunday before she died.

It's not Keith's middle name but it could still be what she called him. Moretti said there were no unknown numbers on her phone and no trace of her arranging to meet someone on Sunday. If it was Keith, they might have bumped into each other in town and arranged to meet Sunday evening. They wouldn't need to call or send messages.

For the next two days it rains. The gargoyles on the bank scream into the wet. Paul Wheeler hasn't made contact again. The police won't investigate him for the assault fifteen years ago. I have to think of a way to prevent him from doing it to someone else. Immobilize him, somehow. I have time. His brother bought him a flat in Leeds, he has a job, he has parole requirements. I doubt he will leave.

Every so often I walk down Bray Lane, but nothing seems out of order in their house. I wait for Natasha to call me. She must be curious. She must want to know the reasons for my suspicion.

⇒ 43 ⇐

Lewis wants to meet at the Cherwell. I don't ask if something has happened with the case. If it had, he wouldn't wait until this afternoon to tell me. Still, on the walk through Oxford to the river, my pulse beats quickly and my legs are light, as though something is about to happen.

"It's closed," he says when I find him outside the pub, and without discussion we circle around the boathouse to the towpath. We walk toward Magdalen and one of the pubs along the river.

"You aren't wearing a suit."

"No," he says. He wears narrow trousers, a white thermal shirt, and a hooded canvas jacket. The path narrows and he walks in front of me. I look at the hood draped between his shoulders, and it's comforting, it reminds me of something but I don't know what.

The river sweeps under a row of fat curved bridges. Underneath them, the sound of our footsteps clatters around us. We go into the first pub, but it's crowded with students from a rugby tournament. On a shelf is a row of bottles of dandelion and burdock. I remember the tennis court, and the sunshine pouring over the town. That day, when Rachel left me at a table next to the inn and went to Keith's house, I want to know what was in her head.

"Should we stop here?" asks Lewis.

"No, let's keep walking." Fog wraps the trees on the opposite bank. Water drips from Magdalen Bridge, making rings on the surface. I watch one of the rings grow wider and bump Lewis's shoulder.

We get coffees at a café with no other customers and one million chairs. Halfway across the room Lewis stops with his hands at his waist and says, "It's a trap." When we finally reach the table I suggested by the window, we look back at all the chairs and become hysterical. I learn that he completely loses it when he laughs.

"I listened to your music," I say. "It was really good."

The band name was Easy Tiger. It wasn't really a band, though, it was just him, playing different instruments. The songs reminded me of Beach House and Blood Orange, and I feel bad for him because he recorded them ten years ago, he would have been right in there with them, if not ahead.

"Who did the vocals?"

"My sister."

She had a lovely, haunting voice. Listening to the songs was difficult, since they filled me with so much longing. One of them was the exact sensation of driving on the Westway late at night.

We spend the rest of the day together, walking down the river and up again through the colleges, and end up at a trattoria on Fetter Lane. We share a split portion of pasta carbonara and one of linguine, and a liter of red wine. We are seated in the bow window facing the narrow cobbled lane.

It was dusk when we arrived, in the lull between seatings, and even though it's now dark there isn't any formality between us. Both of us were starving, and we don't speak at all when the food first arrives.

"Are you leaving soon?" he asks.

"I can't yet."

Something ripples between us. I sit up in my seat and Lewis tips his head back. He lets the silence grow taut.

I almost ruined it. Days of effort and waiting. Keith is close now too, I can tell. The way he looks at me now is different even than it was a few days ago.

"I'm not ready to go back," I say, finally.

"You don't know it's him."

I look away from Lewis to the reflection on the window. Our waiter across the room, the bottle in his hand, the twisting red rope of wine falling from it.

"Tell me about the chief inspector."

"She's brilliant."

We continue talking in this vein, and it's nice, like we're former colleagues. When we leave, the door to the trattoria blows shut and seals it behind us. Lewis asks if I want a ride home, but I want to say good-bye here and not in her town, so I tell him I have to meet a friend nearby. He hugs me. We stay like that, and I sag against him. He holds his hand against the back of my head. It's a relief, like something wrinkled has been smoothed. Then it's over, and he walks to his car by the river and I walk to St. Aldate's and the bus.

➤ 44 ◄

I return to Marlow at half past eight and by habit walk down Bray Lane. There are police cars in front of his house. My gait changes, like I have grown larger, bulkier. My shoulders rise behind my ears. The front door is open, and two uniformed officers are standing in the corridor. One of them steps forward to stop me from entering. He pins my arms and drags me down to the road. A second officer, younger than the first, follows, saying, "He can't hear you, he isn't in there."

The older officer releases me at the edge of the property. I recognize both men, detective constables from Abingdon, and know how weary of me they are, how beside the point it is for them to answer my questions.

"He isn't here," says the younger one. "You're screaming for nothing." I shove him. He turns away and I shove him from behind so he stumbles. The older one clasps my arms at my waist until his partner has entered the house.

The yew trees at the end of Bray Lane shudder up and down with every step. I lick my lips. My breathing is loud in my ears and I walk unsteadily, like my feet are far from me, until I am in the hall at the Hunters. At the bottom of the stairs, my knees give out.

"We're in a very sensitive time," says Moretti. "We still have many hours of interviewing ahead of us. We had grounds to make an arrest, but I can't give you any further information yet."

"If you don't tell me why you arrested him, I'll give an interview to the papers. I have the number for a journalist at the *Telegraph*."

"We've already alerted the media that we arrested a suspect. They'll have learned who by now, and we're going to ask anyone with information about the murder to come forward."

"Why would he do it?"

"As soon as we pass the case to the Crown

Prosecution Service, a solicitor will present the evidence against the suspect to you."

"When?"

"The earliest will be about a week from now. It depends on our interviews, and the continuing inquiry."

One more train will leave for London before they stop running for the night. The high street is deserted but the lights are still on at the newsagent's shop. I choose a bottle of mineral water for the sake of having something to carry up to the till.

"Why are the police at the Denton house?" I ask.

"His wife called them," says Giles. His voice is rough and he seems to have a hard time forming the words. "She found pictures of Rachel."

"Where is she?"

"She's gone to stay with her mum."

"Where?"

"Margate."

⇾ 45 ⇽

To reach Margate, I have to take the train to London, then the tube across the city, then a second train from King's Cross. I don't trust myself to drive. There are five stops to King's Cross. I know each one and before each one I plan to get out. It's over, really. The police have arrested someone. I'm done. I'm free now to, for example, leave at Edgware Road and ride the bus down to Fulham Broadway. Or switch trains and go to the cinema at Notting Hill Gate. Or leave at Chancery Lane and buy a carafe of red wine at the cellar under Furnival Street.

She isn't watching. It makes no difference to her if I pour fuel on his house and set it on fire. It doesn't matter. I could celebrate that the police arrested a suspect by going to the top of the Barbican and jumping. I could celebrate that the police arrested a suspect by going to the Battersea Dogs and Cats Home and adopting a dog. Neither will change what he did to her four weeks ago.

As far as I know. Maybe the moment I land on the road below the Barbican we will go back in time. Maybe when I start the adoption paperwork Rachel will come into the office, rubbing her hands on her jeans, and slide onto the seat next to mine and say, "Have they done all his jabs yet?"

Keith Denton is in custody, but the trial might not occur, or the jury might not convict him. Even if it does he might get a reduced sentence, he'll likely get out while I'm still alive. Especially if the prosecutor can't prove that he planned it. I don't know if the knife belonged to Rachel or if he brought it to her house. What he did to the dog, though, that must be taken into consideration, and every time he comes up for parole the review board will see photographs of it.

By the time the train arrives in Margate, I am drawn and exhausted. The station is on the edge of the city, and I shoulder my bag and walk along the main road to an old-fashioned seaside hotel. I climb three flights of a velvet staircase, gripping a key, which will lead me to a bed. With the window cracked open, I can smell the sea.

I've never been here before. Paul can't know where I am now, I realize. I pull the heavy curtain around my back to block the reflection of the room, and a view of Margate opens past the window. Pastel houses with tar roofs, blurry sodium lights, the sea in the distance. Strange that this city exists, that it would have existed tonight even if I hadn't come.

Her murderer is in custody. He is in a cell, and before I fall asleep I imagine saying to Rachel, It's time, and leading her down a hallway, and turning a key, and letting her inside with him. She's dressed simply and she isn't carrying a weapon, but she doesn't need one. She will be able to tear him apart with her bare hands.

Natasha's mother came to stay with them for a few weeks after the birth of their second son, and during her visit she and Giles chatted sometimes, he told me. Her name is Diane Eaves. Giles didn't have her address, but it's listed.

As soon as I wake, I find the bus route to her

house on the city's outskirts. Before the next one leaves, I walk toward the coast. The town smells of tar and salt, and a thin fog blows in from the sea. Ramshackle terraced houses and fishermen's pubs line the roads. Nearly everyone I see is a teenager or in their twenties or thirties, and it reminds me of the part of Edinburgh near the art school. Tequila, doner kebabs, a dance studio.

I reach the water, flat and dreary, the Margate sands sweeping an exhausting, defeating distance to the break line. The beach huts are very nice. Each one painted a different color, possibly by one of the art students I walked past. A thick bank of fog pours in from the water.

Will they let Keith sleep? Did they interview him overnight? I imagine that now, Moretti, who always looks tired, won't look tired. After sixteen hours with a suspect in custody, he will carry himself as though he could continue on indefinitely.

I find a place on the harbor wall. I don't want to go talk to his wife, and I won't be able to look at her. She repulses me. After what he did, she shared a house with him.

At the end of the pier, a cannon points toward the fog, as though at any moment a ship might appear. I can't remember who invaded this stretch of coastline. Along with the cannon, I watch the swirling fog, listen for the splash of waves against a hull, wait for a bowsprit.

Whatever happens now, I can still punish him.

I can drive his dog into the woods and set her loose. I can collect his sons from primary school. Hello, I'm a friend of your mum's, do you want to stop for ninety-nines on the way home? Keith would never know if they were alive or not, or where they had gone.

I board a bus bound south toward Ramsgate. As I walk down the aisle, the bus stirs, and the shops and houses of Margate begin to scroll by backward to either side.

Natasha Denton's mum lives in a subdivision near the main road. The houses are small boxes of white plaster with low clay roofs. Ragged brown palm trees blow in the gardens. Television aerials bob up and down.

Natasha opens the door and at once I feel deluded, appearing on her doorstep so far from where she lives. She stares at a point on one of the roofs behind me. "I'll get my coat. I don't want her to listen," she says, nodding into the house.

She doesn't speak until we round the corner. "After you came to see me, I went through his phone. I almost told him, I wanted to apologize. I didn't have to search the house, the police already had weeks ago. They turned the place upside down.

"The boys liked to play with a loose tile in our bathroom when they were younger. When you slide it off, there's a little cave behind it. The police couldn't have known. I almost convinced myself not to check, and I waited all afternoon before looking. There were photographs of her.

"I brought the pictures to my friend's house before I asked him about them. Wasn't that clever? I thought he might try to burn them. He started to cry and said they had an affair but he didn't hurt her and he didn't know who did. He said he loved her. He asked if I was going to call the police and I said no because of the boys and then he went to work and I called the police."

"Did you suspect him before?"

"No. You look so much like her. When I saw you just now, I thought you were her. I thought you had come to punish me."

"She wouldn't punish you."

"Oh, I think she would," she says. "She'd be furious."

"Was Keith in any of the pictures?"

"No. I asked if he stole them and he said no. He got quite angry that I suggested it. We were in the kitchen and I remember looking at the knives and thinking he wouldn't stab me. He couldn't be bothered, with me."

"Has he ever been violent in the past?"

"No, but he has a temper."

I planned to tell her that he hit me, but it doesn't seem necessary. She's already disgusted by him. "Was there anything else?"

"After we heard about the murder, he asked me

the last time I saw Rachel. It was just passing on the aqueduct, but he wanted to know everything about it. What she was wearing, what she said, where she was going. I thought he was in shock."

A woman pushes a pram toward us, and after she passes, Natasha says, "We'll have to change our names. I don't want the boys growing up with this."

"That's probably wise."

I'm not sure of the way out of the subdivision, so she leads me back to the main road, as though through a maze. I wait for the bus into Margate. Natasha told me she was going to move, maybe abroad, for her sons. I wonder if any part of her finds this thrilling. She didn't give the impression of having been particularly happy and now she can start over, find a different life that suits her better. The normal obligations don't weigh on her anymore. I imagine her in the weeks before this thinking, Is this it? Is this how things will always be? And now the answer is no.

⇒ 46 ⇐

I take the train back to London the next morning. What at night was rounded and storybook (shape of barn, shape of tree) is now sodden, thin, and colorless. The fields are pale, the house paint faded against the bleached sky. After we pass

Faversham, I call Lewis. "His wife thinks he did it," I say.

"Yes, she does. It looks like we're going to charge him, Nora."

I wonder if the police have told my dad about the arrest. I hope they won't be able to find him again. I don't think I will be able to bear helping him in and out of the courtroom, watching him shuffle to his seat. I have a surge of anger then. Where's my family? I think. Where's *my* family?

The detectives and a solicitor from the Crown Prosecution Service will assemble the case against Keith Denton. Lewis says the case will move to trial only if the prosecution has an excellent chance of winning.

The next few days will be spent examining any weaknesses in the evidence, he says, and searching out possible defenses. The police will review the circumstances around the crime, the details that are not relevant to the trial but will help win the confidence of the jury. When they finish, the prosecutor will decide if the case will go to trial.

I decide to wait for the news in Marlow, and the prospect turns me restless. In a room in Abingdon someone is going to sit down with a file and decide what happens next. I can't go talk to this person. I can't plead with her.

At the Hunters, I find the names of the dozen prosecutors in Oxford who might have been assigned to her case, and consider approaching them. Their stakes are different from ours. I wonder how many cases Oxford CPS brings to trial every year. What would losing one mean? A bad day, a drink after work, at worst, a professional review.

None of their addresses are listed. They must not want certain people to know where they live. But I could follow them home from the CPS office or Abingdon police station. I imagine the thud of a car door, their polished shoes tapping on the walk, and following them through the open gate, saying, Excuse me.

They wouldn't listen, and my desperation might only make things worse. I can't do anything for her. I remember her weight in my arms. The hours drag by. They have seven days to decide. Lewis is going to call me with the decision, and I try not to see portents everywhere.

Lewis calls me in the evening.

"Have they made a decision?"

"No, it's something else," he says. "The chief inspector has agreed to release her body. You can call the coroner to make arrangements."

➤ 47 ⬥

The drive takes six hours, and by the time I reach Polperro it is dark. I park on a steep, narrow road behind the Crumplehorn Inn and collect the box of ashes from the footwell. I wish we had done this differently, with a coffin and pallbearers. I shouldn't be able to lift the box on my own, but I can, and then I am carrying it down the cobbled streets to the Green Man, a lime-washed inn by the harbor where I will spend the night.

At dawn tomorrow I will scatter the ashes in the cove below the house we rented. I chose Cornwall because it is where she intended to go, five weeks ago. She had already rented a flat on the other side of the county. I have the address in St. Ives, but I think seeing it might tip me over some last, final barricade, and I don't know what things would be like afterward.

I can't manage to think of them as her ashes. Instead the box is something she has entrusted to my care, and I am scared something will happen to me before I can complete the errand. On the M5 I thought I would crash and now, as I turn the corner and the Green Man comes into view, I am sure it will burn down with us inside. It wouldn't be the worst thing. Her ashes would still end up in the ocean, floating with the cinders in long fingers of smoke over the sea.

• • •

Before dawn, I carry the box along the flagged stones of the quay. In the inner harbor, the tide is in, and sailing boats rock on the silvery water, their rigging clinking against the masts. The slate roofs seem to glow in the darkness. The sky is just beginning to lighten at the horizon as I circle around the inner harbor, and I can see the black outline of the two umbrella pines.

I climb the coast path along the edge of the headland. At its highest point I turn to look back at Polperro. More lights have come on, and smoke curls from the chimneys. I look at the fisherman's croft, nearly invisible against the rocks, and at the two square merchant's houses. One white, the other tweed-brown, though in this light the white one is blue, and the tweed one black.

The sand of the path crunches beneath my boots. Wind rustles the low sage pines on the headland. The coast doesn't look very different from in summer, since so much of it is evergreen. I listen to the boom of the waves at the base of the cliff.

After a half mile, the coast path curves around a familiar white oak. Its branches creak with a sound like a door opening.

Another, shorter stretch and then a house comes into view, set down from the path by the edge of the cliff. Our house! I worried it wouldn't be here anymore.

The house is empty. The man who owns it

spends most of the year in London. There are still colored buoys hanging from a tree at the edge of the property. There is the outdoor shower, its spigot foxed with mold, its crooked door on the latch. And the clothesline, a wire strung between two whitewashed poles. In this light the wire is invisible, the pegs floating in midair against the sea. I remember pegging up my swimsuit, with wet hair, wearing a blue dress sprigged with white flowers.

The sense of recognition propels me forward until I stand on the back porch, facing the sea, and then it begins to fracture, so while I am surveying the house, I am also worrying about the prosecutor's decision, and I am pleading for Rachel's life, and I am thinking about how we planned to come back here. We wanted to come back for years and years, until we were both old.

The staircase vanishes down the cliff to the sea, and I imagine that Rachel is climbing the steps. Forty years on. The sea below her, the rivulets in the cliff. A formidable old woman, with her hair wet from an early swim. She puts her hand on the railing and leans back to check if she can see her sister, her children, her grandchildren, if any of them has come to the edge of the lawn to wait for her.

I cross the damp lawn and carry the box down the seventy-one steps to the beach. I remove my shoes and socks. I wait until the sun comes over the eastern headland, then twist the lid from the box and walk to the edge of the surf. The icy water stings my skin and soaks through my jeans. I throw handfuls of ash into the water. There is little wind and the things that I worried might happen do not. Most of the ash sinks below the water and the particles that float on the surface are soon roiled by the next wave. Sunlight floods the cove and the waves and the few offshore clouds with color. It takes me a while to recognize that what I feel is disappointment. I had hoped so much for a signal from her.

When I finish, I kneel to rinse my hands and the box in the water. I hold my hands in the clear cold water for longer than necessary, until long after the last of the ash is rinsed away.

On the porch, I use a glove to wipe the sand and water from my blue feet. I pull on woolen socks and roll my sodden jeans down over them. My teeth chatter. My mind is blank. She's gone.

I zip my coat to my chin and rock back and forth. I am so cold that I go around the house to the outdoor shower. How good it would feel to take off my wet socks and jeans and stand under a jet of steaming water. I twist the tap but nothing happens. The water must be shut off to keep the pipes from freezing.

I return to the porch, which has the most sun. The day will grow warmer as it rises. Behind me are the rooms where she slept for three weeks, the rooms where she cooked, the rooms where she read. During our trip, Rachel was reading Clarice Lispector and I was alternating between John Fowles and the soggy detective novels in the cabinet under the stairs. Every morning one of us walked to the bakery for almond croissants and I ate mine here with my book. I broke the horn of the croissant and licked out the marzipan. Ahead of me, trenches of ocean rose and fell for miles.

At night I watched the stars from the hammock and was scared by the size of the universe as I hadn't been since I was little. Rachel climbed in next to me, tucking my socked feet under her arm, pulling a blanket over her chest, and the two of us stared out.

It was good to be so scared. The ocean was very large, as was the universe. Which contained the ocean. And the oceans on other planets, and other planets. The fear made the domestic rituals better. The almond croissant, the detective novel, the outdoor shower. Here I am, I thought, taking an outdoor shower in the universe.

While we were here, I wanted to stay forever, but I was also already thinking of leaving. Always biding and always going, always at the exact same time.

"What's your favorite thing about Cornwall?" I asked her, but it wasn't what I meant, I meant what's your favorite thing about being alive.

➤ 48 ➤

In Polperro, birds wheel over the masts of boats in the inner harbor. On the decks, a few men smoke as they ready their boats for the day, and I listen to their voices and the rigging clinking. I decide to stay in Cornwall for the next four days. There is no reason to return to Oxford until the prosecutor's decision, and their deadline is five days from now.

For the next four days, I acted as though I were still scattering her ashes, and should visit only the places here she loved best. This meant a lot of driving.

I visited the rivers Fowey, Fal, and Helford. I ate at St. John's in Fowey at sunset, as the windows across the estuary in Polruan became shimmering brass squares. I ordered what she would have ordered, which was rainbow trout. The drink was more difficult, and from her three favorites I chose a white Bordeaux.

I visited Frenchman's Creek. I visited the fishing town of Cadgwith. I tried to find the falls she had talked about on the Lizard Peninsula, but couldn't. It may have dried up. No one I asked had heard of a dark pink lighthouse either. She may have told me the wrong color, or I remembered it wrong. I visited Porthgwidden and found the stall where she bought buttered crumpets.

I visited Redruth. I visited Lostwithiel and Padstow. I rode the ferry across the bay. This was a pattern I could follow for the rest of my life. I could retrace her steps. I could visit the hostel where she stayed in Greece and try to track down the man she met there. She lost his number when she was on the train north, which she always said was a blessing in disguise, but maybe it wasn't.

One by one I could replace my tastes with hers. I don't like mussels, for example, but I ordered them in a restaurant she liked in Cadgwith and finished the bowl. I could sleep with the men she would have slept with. I could become a nurse, even. It's not like I already have a career.

And maybe that's what I would do, if she were in prison. If what happened that day was that she killed someone instead of the other way around. I would do what she wanted me to and then tell her about it in detail. We often confused memories. It was easy if you talked for long enough.

On my last night, I visited Mousehole, and on the drive back it began to snow. It almost never snows in Cornwall, and I held my breath, hoping it wouldn't stop. I drove over hills, across the peninsula.

At the edge of a town I hadn't seen before was an old-fashioned Esso station, the two narrow pumps, the glowing lozenges atop them. Snow drifted over the empty filling station. The road was wet and black along its center and white at its edges, where the snow hadn't been touched. The gothic spires of a church tower were almost invisible against the night sky. The glowing sign for a garage stood beside the filling station, and other signs—RAC Repairer, Community House—hung from wrought-iron hooks on the edges of the buildings. An old car sat with its headlights, two orbs mounted on the round wells of its tires, switched on.

As soon as I cross the bridge over the river Tamar, I want to turn back. I want to keep drifting around Cornwall. It would be a happy life. I could visit Frenchman's Creek in a thunderstorm. I could find the dark pink lighthouse. After a heavy rain, a falls will appear somewhere on the Lizard Peninsula. A sudden fan of silver water, spraying between the green headlands, twisting down the side of a black ravine.

I could order the scallops at St. John's. They were her second choice, and she had a hard time deciding.

The bridge span rattles under the tires. Far below, chunks of ice and snow float on the water. Ahead of me is the Devon side. I want to stay in Cornwall, but Rachel was not arrested, she isn't in prison, and I will never be able to feed her my memories.

As I drive east, the calm of the past four days is replaced by dread. The prosecutors will announce their decision tomorrow. I keep thinking that I need to call someone to make sure that the charge isn't lowered from murder to manslaughter. I keep doing the maths based on the different minimum sentence lengths, to find out how old he will be when he gets out, how old I will be.

I drive toward Keith Denton's house. I pretend that someone knows where I am. I pretend I have been trained and somewhere the people who trained me are standing in a great stone house, thin women in black suits with cigarettes and men smoking cigars and looking out the window at the rain, my spymasters, my superintendents.

⇸ 49 ⇷

The shingled house appears empty. Natasha and the two boys are likely still in Margate, and Keith is at the station in Abingdon, unless they moved him to the nick in Oxford. The dog didn't come to the door in Margate, I wonder if they kenneled her or if Natasha has already given her away to punish him.

A stain spreads across the gravel below where he parked the van. I stand for a long time looking down at it, though I know I'm being ridiculous, it can't be her blood. The stain must be fuel or motor oil. I crouch down and lift a handful of gravel, which has the sharp scent of petrol.

When I am halfway up the drive, a man comes out of the house next door, and we stare at each other. He is about forty. He has a shaved head and wears an anorak. I recognize him from town, though I don't know where. He shifts his weight, watching me. After a few moments, he continues down to the road. I let my breath out. I wonder if he would have stopped me if Keith were at home, or if I were carrying a hammer wrapped in plastic.

Once the neighbor turns on Redgate, I continue to the front door. I open the letter box and sort through the past few days of post. Nothing personal has arrived for Keith, no envelopes with handwritten addresses. I decide to continue checking it while he is in custody, on the slight chance that something useful might arrive.

There is not much to look at in his garden. A shed, a cherry tree, which in spring will froth with white or pink blossom. In one corner is a stack of boxes, and I pull the drawers open. An apiary, of all things. I consider the dry honey-combs and the white resin and imagine him showing up at Rachel's house with a stupid grin and a chunk of fresh, dripping honeycomb wrapped in paper. "Just thought you might like it." I open one of the drawers and spit in it.

One of them left a recycling bin by the back door. The police must have gone through his rubbish weeks ago, and I wonder if they searched it again after arresting him. Bottles of white wine and cans of Strongbow. No Tennent's Light Ale. No proof yet that he watched her from the ridge. I replace the bottles and cans gently, to avoid attracting the neighbors' attention.

They had an affair, or he fixated on her, or some combination of the two. He stalked her. He watched her from the ridge, and offered to do jobs at her house, and stole the photographs. He wasn't in any of them, which would make them strange mementos of a relationship.

I cup my hands around my eyes and look through a window. The kitchen clearly belongs to a family. If they did have an affair, Rachel would never have come here.

There would be plenty of other meeting places. They would meet at isolated countryside inns or at hotels in London, even in Oxford. I imagine them setting off at different times down the aqueduct and, far from the village, after the hazel copse, stumbling off the path and pressing against a tree.

I can imagine her in an affair but not with him. He doesn't fit the role. I can't imagine her doing anything risky or desperate for him, and she would hate him for betraying his wife.

The more I think about it, the more I think she isn't the type for any of it, not the subterfuge, not the narcotic obsession of an affair. Other people's delusions disgusted her.

Alice had an affair with one of our teachers, and I can't imagine Rachel doing any of what she did, walking by his house, for example, and seeing that he was home with his family and telling him to meet her around the corner and fuck her in her car. The teacher was crazy about her. Alice put an end to it, and he said, "But we were going to go to the beach together." I felt sorry for him, but Rachel didn't. "Sad fuck," she said. She didn't understand why he insisted on lying to his wife instead of leaving.

I think Rachel made Keith feel foolish. I think she made him feel foolish at a point when he couldn't recover from it, he had hoped for too much. He proposed something to her and she laughed or told him off, and it was too late, she was already precious to him.

He came home afterward, I think. He showered and washed his clothes. It would seem safer to do here than anywhere else. He must have left traces everywhere, in the pipes, in the floorboards. The police didn't look hard enough for evidence. It is there somewhere, in the pipes, and they should have torn the house apart to get to it.

Before I leave the property, I return to the shed for the secateurs and trim the cherry tree until there is not much of it left.

I go to the Duck and Cover, but there isn't any news. The bartender tells me that as far as anyone knows Keith has not been released. Snow begins to fall on the town, and we both turn to watch it. It falls heavily, not like in Cornwall. The half-timbered houses across the road look, for a moment, ancient, and the people on the pavement have the defined features and heavy gazes of people in old paintings. Their eyes are dark and serious as they look up and across the road toward us, to see what the snow has already done, what it will go on to do.

➤ 50 ➤

At the library the next morning I take down a contemporary French novel about a woman who murders her doctor. It is the sort of thing I've been avoiding. She stabs him. But I read it anyway, standing in the library, then sitting. Somehow, it's like an antidote.

The narrator lives next to the Gare de l'Est. She commits the crime on the rue de la Clef. She returns the knife to her old flat in the sixième. The story is brisk and clean in a way that seems particularly French. I hope she gets away with it.

I worry the librarian, the boy with the round glasses, will not let me borrow it. He will look at it and say, You shouldn't be reading this.

This does not happen. I carry the novel home and finish it in my room. Near the end, I realize I have been picturing the narrator as Rachel.

I am reading certain parts of the book again—the part at the Gare du Nord, the part at the coliseum —when Lewis calls and asks me to come downstairs. This was not what I planned to be doing when he called with the prosecutor's decision. I planned to be outdoors, for one thing. Instead I am reading about a woman disposing of evidence in the Seine.

A cold weight settles in my stomach. I dress in clean clothes and braid my hair, as though it will help to look respectable and compliant.

I walk down the carpeted stairs and past the painting of the red riders. My heart thumps against my ribs. Lewis waits for me on the road, leaning against an unmarked car. His face is blank and I wait for it to shift. I hug my jumper to my chest against the wind.

"Nora," he says, and I know from his voice. "CPS isn't going to prosecute Keith Denton."

"But he was there. He stole photographs of her. He doesn't have an alibi."

"It's not enough. We have no forensic evidence against him."

Lewis opens the car door for me. Through the windscreen, I watch him walk around to the driver's side, a tall, handsome man in a long coat, and wonder if he is savoring these few seconds alone before he has to rejoin me.

He doesn't turn on the engine. There is nowhere to go. I don't have to speak to a prosecutor or attend his appearance before a magistrate, though I don't know if those are things I would have done if this had gone the way it should have.

"Where is he?"

"I don't know. He was released early this morning from St. Aldate's."

I resist the urge to turn around in my seat. "Did you check the drains at his house?"

"Yes, when we first interviewed him."

"What are you going to do?" I ask.

"If we don't find any new evidence, the inquiry will lose priority."

"Has that already started?"

"Yes. Our resources are limited at the moment," he says, which means there has been another murder near Abingdon.

"Is it related?"

"No. Two men were killed at a warehouse in Eynsham. It appears to be a hate crime."

Moretti will solve the case quickly, I think. A sop to his conscience.

"Can you charge him again? Or does he have immunity now?"

"We can, with compelling new evidence," he says. "But it doesn't happen often."

Keith was released hours ago. I might have

bumped into him on leaving the library, when I thought he was in custody. The thought makes me laugh. Lewis runs his hand over his eyes.

"Do you think he did it?" I ask.

"I don't know."

I want him to say yes, even though it will only add to my fury. Was it laziness, on the part of the prosecutors? Did they not want to increase their caseload? Or was it money, are there too few courts and judges in this country? When I say this aloud, Lewis says, "Or it's a moral decision not to make an innocent man endure a trial."

"What's your instinct about him?"

"Based on what?" His voice sounds tense and strangled. I wonder if he was in Eynsham| last night, and what he saw.

"If you were forced to decide—"

"Nora, I don't know." His head rests on his hand. "You shouldn't speak to him. He's trying to get an order of protection against you."

It will never be solved now. Not formally, anyway, not with a conviction. There won't be a trial. The detectives in Abingdon are in the first forty-eight hours of a new case. Lewis will leave soon, and Moretti will take the early retirement scheme. Both of them will be gone before the new year is out, I think. Not because of Rachel. I don't think any of the officers will be haunted by her. I wish they would be, then there might be a chance of one of them solving it. The strange thing is this probably isn't the worst case any of them has seen, or the saddest. They will carry other people with them into the future. Children, probably.

Keith Denton is free. I imagine him coming home and setting the house to rights after its two sudden departures. I wonder if he made a list of the things he would do as a free man. Pint of bitter, walk in the hills.

The exonerated man. His friends and the town will rally around him. They will want to hear all about his narrow escape. Everyone knows the system is cracked. At least some of the thousands of people in prison for murder are innocent, and he almost became one of them. The town will be happy to believe he is innocent. Better a stranger than someone who has been inside their own homes.

⇸ 51 ⇷

I sit at one of the wooden tables next to the Hunters and listen to the news on my headphones. A few words stream by that I don't catch, and I try to work out what the reporter might have said. I'm so absorbed it takes me a few seconds to realize what is in front of me. Keith coming around the corner of the building.

I tug my headphones off and he slumps onto the bench across from me. A tinny voice leaks from the headphones but I don't switch the radio off, as though the person on the other line will be listening if anything happens to me. His hands are in his pockets, and I can't tell if he has a weapon. At the moment we are out of view of anyone on the high street.

"You killed her," I say, and my voice doesn't sound like me, it sounds like her.

He shakes his head, either to warn me to stop talking or to correct me. "Do you want to know what I can't figure out?" he says, staring at the join in the wood. "They never thought about you."

"I don't know what you mean."

"You were in the house with Rachel. The police arrive, you're waiting outside, covered in her blood, and they don't arrest you."

"I found her."

"If you found her you would want to get away from the house. You'd run to the neighbors or down the road. You wouldn't wait around, in case whoever did it was still inside. Unless it was you."

"I wasn't thinking clearly at that point," I say. Keith's body is oddly slack, like he can't hold himself up properly.

"One of the firemen told me he was watching you, and he said you didn't cry. And there's the dog. I can't get my head around it. What you're saying is an intruder, someone breaking into the house, killed a trained German shepherd. I don't know how you could do that without serious injuries, but whoever it was didn't lose any blood."

"How do you know that?"

"I'm guessing. They didn't ask for my blood. I think you slit the dog's throat while he was sleeping."

"The police eliminated me." I remember Moretti asking if it was normal for me to be at the house at that time. He considered me as a suspect.

"How?"

"I don't know. I didn't have a weapon."

"Did Rachel have any knives in her kitchen? You either washed it or hid it afterward." He lifts his head. "They're coming for you now. They know what you did, and they know why you did it."

"I'd never hurt her."

"Would you throw a bottle at her face?"

"How do you know about that?"

He snorts. "How the fuck do you think? What is it about me that makes it so hard for you to believe?"

I shake my head, and he says, "You broke her nose."

I don't argue. It was hard to tell if her nose was broken because of me or what happened to her a few hours later.

"You stole pictures of her."

"No. Rachel gave them to me. She loved me."

He laughs at my expression.

"She always said you were a little bitch."

PART THREE

FOXES

⇥ 52 ⇤

We got in a fight at the party. After we played Nevers, before I climbed the stairs, with everything below my knees a fuzzy darkness. Rachel teased me and I snapped at her and then we were through the back door and screaming at each other on the lawn. Rafe said he was going to call it in to the police as a domestic. He said it as a joke, but then Rachel said something to him about me and I took the beer bottle from his hand and threw it at her. It hit her in the face and she inhaled sharply and bent over.

My stomach soured, but then she looked up and laughed with the blood coursing down her face. Clearly the victor. I'd proved her right. She was still laughing when I retreated inside.

The boys kept us apart for the rest of the night. They made huddles around us and joked with us like we were boxers. They acted impressed but mostly they thought we were both mental, a nightmare, like Ali Ross, who at the last party did all the windows in her boyfriend's car.

Rachel leaned over me, early in the morning. "Nora, do you want to come with me or stay?"

"Stay."

We fought at most of the parties that summer, if one of us drank enough, which we always did, and if we weren't too distracted by trying to pull someone. We fought carelessly, the way our friends fought with their mothers, and mostly over nothing.

Every walk home followed the same idiot logic. First silent bitterness, then recrimination, an echo of before but with less slurring. By the time we reached the old center of town one of us said, I don't want to talk about this anymore. We walked in angry silence past the Norman church and the bakery with our sandals slapping the pavement. Maddening, how our strides joined up even when we didn't want them to. We looked in opposite directions, a gloomy Janus head.

The fourth stage usually started near the end of the high street. One of us made a remark, often about the party, and a stupid thing someone else had done or said at it. This stage involved more recrimination, but also a few very faint apologies, like, I didn't think you'd take it that way.

We would start to get bored. The neon sky and the strangeness of the town at that hour would slowly colonize our attention. By the time we crossed onto the estate, the fight would be over.

I can still see Rachel at seventeen, a line of blood curving over her mouth, laughing at me.

I thought if she went on her own she might think about what she had said about me, and that she would be sorry. It drives me to distraction now, that I can't remember what she said to upset me so much.

➤ 53 ❦

Keith knows about the fight, and he knows Fenno was trained. The simplest explanation for how he knows these things is that she told him. That they had an affair, or a friendship he thought was an affair. The strange thing is, when he came to see me, he acted like the affair proved his innocence. If anything it means the opposite.

The important thing now is that Keith thinks it's over for him. He thinks he's safe. He might think, like I did, that he's protected from being charged again by a form of double jeopardy. It must be such a sense of relief, after nearly going to prison. He will live the rest of his days a free man. I imagine that on the aqueduct he wants to kneel and kiss the ground. In his house, in the pub, driving the roads. He must be making plans now, with all the years he has, plans to travel, to sleep rough.

If someone were to threaten all that, there is no telling what he would do. Or, really, there is. He is going to attack me, and it will look unprovoked to everyone except the two of us.

I want him back with the police. They know how to snare him by letting him mention some detail of the crime—how the dog was tied, where her body was found—that they never told him, or by interviewing him until his account begins to shift and break apart. Even though they didn't manage it before, they need more time with him.

The best way to do this is for him to commit another crime. It shouldn't take very long, someone with a temper like that.

I've never understood why the police don't use bait more often. When someone started to kill women on a mountain in Wales, the police could have sent hikers down the trails. With teams following them, or with guns. They could be policewomen, not civilians. It wasn't even a very large mountain, they could have baited every trail. Eight victims, over three months, and the murderer has never been found. Fucking stupid.

Grievous bodily harm. He's ready for it, too. He needs to take it out on someone.

⇥ 54 ⇤

Moretti gives a press conference from a room inside Abingdon station. He asks for anyone who was near the warehouse in Eynsham on Thursday night to make contact with the police. He says that based on early evidence they believe more than one person was responsible for the murders, and he urges anyone with information, however minor, to come forward.

He's done with Rachel. It's over for him, unless another development draws him back.

A row of detectives sits beside him behind low, angled microphones. While he speaks, the officers stare at the press audience with blank, judging faces, as though waiting for an outburst. Based on the crowns on their epaulets, some of them are his superiors. I recognize the chief constable, seated near the middle of the row with his hands clasped on the table.

Moretti's voice is measured and clear. The impression he gives is of someone who is serious and, more than anything, effective.

⇥ 55 ⇤

"Can you come to the station?" asks Moretti the morning after the press conference. Rain falls on the yard behind the Hunters, and the foghorn bellows from the village hall. I remember what Keith said about the police suspecting me, but I don't believe him. It was a bluff. I'm pleased the detectives haven't closed the inquiry.

A constable collects me at a quarter past eight. This time Lewis is also in the interview room. For a moment I think this must mean there is news, but neither of them looks eager. They look exhausted.

"Why did your last relationship end?" asks Moretti.

"He was unfaithful."

"How did you know?"

"I found a pair of knickers. I told you already."

On the Sunday night of his return from Manchester, I reached into his bag and pulled out a fistful of black silk. I spread them flat on the bed to see the dimensions of the body that wore them. The legs and stomach that the lace edged. I imagined a woman lying on her back, topless, biting her finger and laughing.

Moretti shows me a photograph of a pair of black silk knickers, with the same faint blue label stitched to the hem.

"Like these?"

"Yes."

"They have a shop on the Via Cavour in Rome. They don't distribute abroad." I've stopped breathing. Both detectives watch me. Moretti says, "When did you find out?"

"Find out what?"

"That Rachel slept with your boyfriend."

"She didn't. He was in Manchester that weekend."

"No, Oxford. He stayed at the George on Prince Street. Rachel met him for dinner and she stayed with him at the hotel."

The first kick lands. My body turns numb, as it did on that Sunday night. I'm very aware of my movements, of lifting my hand to straighten my shirt, of how much air I displace in the room, as though everything around me is freezing up. It's not unpleasant. Lewis watches from across the table. He still hasn't spoken.

"How many times?" I ask. My voice telescopes away from me.

"Once, according to Liam," says Moretti.

I startle, as though I have been pushed from behind. "He's admitted it?"

"Yes."

I look at the photograph and remember placing them on our bed and smoothing the cool silk. Liam was in the shower and I left them like that for him to find.

"Thank you, Nora. That's all we need for today."

He hasn't turned off the recorder. I wonder what else he thinks I might say.

⇒ 56 ⇐

"Can you come to Oxford now?" I ask at the first pause in his condolences.

"I'm at work," says Liam.

"I'm sure you can explain. The train's only an hour, you can be back in London tonight."

We arrange to meet at the covered market on the high street. There is a bistro on the second floor. It serves good, rustic French food, though I'm not hungry.

Moretti might be trying to find a motive for me.

He may have ordered the knickers from the shop in Rome, not found a matching pair in Rachel's dresser. I think I told him the brand name.

While I wait for Liam, I sort through all the times I saw them together. A few times the two of them went off on their own. But they were always on ordinary, reasonable two-person jobs. They once did the grocery shopping when we stayed in Marlow, or he drove her to collect her car from the repair garage.

It hurts too much to believe that these expeditions were planned, and eagerly awaited. When they returned, they never seemed tense or guilty.

Moretti never showed me any proof that Liam was in Oxford and not Manchester. He didn't say how he knew that Rachel stayed at the hotel.

Liam arrives. I haven't seen him in six months. He wears a soft black jumper and he smells the same, a cologne with cedar and musk that I realized was quite popular after we broke up. Who do you wear it for now? I think before I can stop myself.

"How are you?" he asks.

I shake my head, and then notice the magazine folded in his briefcase. He was able to read on the trip here, and I hate him for it. The server comes and I order a second Campari and soda. Liam orders a beer. He looks so well.

"Did you sleep with my sister?"

Everything around us goes quiet.

"Yes."

I swipe his bottle and it shatters against the wall. The liquid foams and spills along the floor. The two servers, both young women, stop at the far end of the room and stare. I doubt they heard our conversation, but they can imagine it. Both of their faces are creased with sympathy. I push back my chair and hurry down the stairs. Behind me I can hear Liam apologizing, a zip on his case opening as he searches for notes to leave on the table.

He catches me up in the alley beside the covered market. "It wasn't planned. We ran into each other on the street and decided to eat together later. I don't even remember it," he says. "Neither of us did. It was a mistake."

"How much did you drink?"

"Two bottles of wine."

"Each?" I ask, scrupulous, desperate. If it happened after four bottles of wine, I might be able to forgive them.

"No, together."

We hear footsteps at the far end of the alley and stop speaking. A young woman comes down the cobbles, teetering between us. She has a net bag with vegetables and a bouquet of tulips, and I almost grab her arm and say, Listen to this, listen to what he's done. She lowers her head demurely as she passes us. Lovers' quarrel. I wish we were having a row, I wish we were in an alley in

London, that there was no reason for us to be in Oxford.

"But you planned it. You told me you were going to Manchester."

"No. I said I was going to a conference. We didn't talk about where until afterward. When I came back, I said I'd been in Manchester."

"Did she ask you to say that?"

"No."

I'm having trouble breathing. I was so sure he would deny it. No, I would tell the detective. You're wrong. It never happened.

And if he denied it I would never have to think about Rachel kissing him, about Rachel undressing for him, about the two of them falling asleep together, or about the first time that I saw her afterward and she didn't tell me. I told her we broke up and she said, "Do you want to come up here for a few days?"

"Did you fancy her the whole time?" I ask.

"No."

"Was she angry with me?"

"No," he says. "No, of course not. She hated herself for it."

I am crying freely now, stoppering my nose with the back of my hand. He looks down at the cobblestones. We don't speak, and then I say, "Are you seeing someone?"

He rubs his hand over his mouth.

"What's her name?"

"Charlotte."

I can picture her. Cheerful and good-natured, shining light brown hair. Going to work and meeting her friends, meeting Liam, afterward. If she were here, if she came toward us now, I would hit her. I would want to claw her to pieces.

She's waiting for him in London. Tonight or tomorrow night he'll go to see her. It will be a relief, after this, to be near someone serene and warm. She'll say, "Do you want to tell me what happened?"

Liam still hasn't realized my position. He hasn't considered the danger he's put me in.

"I found her."

"Oh, God. I'm so sorry."

"They think I killed her because of this."

His throat is flushed red, and it spreads down his chest. "No, that's not possible. I'll tell them you didn't know."

I step forward and his arms close around me. His chest lifts and sinks against mine. I remember the room at the top of the Oxo Tower. Elderflower gin and tonics. I'd thought, I didn't know things could be like this.

He's seeing someone. It can't compare to our first months. Golden brown, lays me down. Even the hotel with Rachel can't compare.

Warmth spreads through his body into mine. He's kissing the top of my head and if I turn my face he will kiss my mouth. He tightens his arms around me. I rest my head between his shoulder and his warm throat and try to ignore the disquiet. It will never be how it was before. This will harm you more, in the end.

"I have to go," I say and my voice sounds calm, like I've just remembered an appointment.

"Will you be all right?" he asks, and I realize that he expects me to say yes.

My voice stays composed as I say good-bye. At the end of the alley, I turn into the crowds on the high street. The loneliness has me by the throat, and I hear Rachel tell me, You're fine, all you have to do now is get home, all you have to do is get home.

⇒ 57 ⇐

"Before leaving London, you went to a pub on Christchurch Terrace in Chelsea," says Moretti. As soon as I left Liam, he called me back to the station. I told him again that I hadn't known about them, but I can't offer any proof. "How much did you have to drink?"

"One glass of wine." I can see the table in front of me, as if I could go back. The salmon in pastry, the white wine, the cutlery.

"What about the night of Rachel's attack in Snaith? How much did you have to drink then?"

"I don't remember."

"Half a liter of vodka?" he asks. I tilt my head. "We spoke to Alice. She said the three of you drank quite a lot that night. Does that sound accurate?"

"Yes."

"Were you angry with Rachel?"

"No."

"You threw a bottle at her face," he says. Keith must have told him. I wonder if he also told them about Liam, if Rachel confessed to him. "Who was Will Cooke?"

Fuck, I think, fuck. "A friend of ours. He went to school with us."

"Was he your friend or Rachel's?"

"Both."

"Was he your boyfriend?"

"For a few months."

"Was he ever Rachel's boyfriend?"

"No."

"That isn't what Alice told us."

"They had sex a few times."

"Was your fight at the party about Will Cooke?"

"No, that wasn't a problem. Did Alice tell you she also slept with Will? We were teenagers, it meant nothing."

When we met, I liked Moretti because I like Italy. How stupid, but it disarmed me. A Scottish accent and Italian appearance. I had an image of him. Drinking an espresso and reading the paper. He has heavy eyelids and I thought that meant he was tortured by his cases and the things he learned in his work. He told me his grandparents owned a bergamot grove in Calabria.

I didn't try to resist. I was so happy that he and Lewis were nothing like the detectives in Snaith. I don't know why he became a policeman. I don't know what he has done in his career, and I don't know if he believes me.

"When did you stop taking Wellbutrin?"

"October."

"Have you had any withdrawal symptoms?"

"No."

"Has it been difficult to resume daily life without the medication?"

"No."

"How many weeks passed between when you stopped the medication and Rachel's death?"

"Five. I don't understand why that's relevant. It's not an antipsychotic."

"What would it mean if it were an antipsychotic?"

"Then going off it might make me violent or unstable."

"And that would mean?"

"That I should be a suspect."

He smiles again. Then he stands and opens the door for me to go. He's not arresting me. I wonder which pieces are still missing, or if it's only the knife.

I stop in the doorway, close to him. "Rachel

had defensive wounds. If I did it, I would have had scratches or bruises."

"Did you?" he asks.

I laugh. "You saw me. You know I didn't."

He shrugs, and the hair stands on the back of my neck.

➤ 58 ✦

I drive to Prince Street. A reconstruction. I can see where they ate dinner. I can ride in one of the lifts, where they probably kissed for the first time, and walk down one of the corridors. Maybe they didn't make it to the room. Both of them liked sex in public, I know.

The George Hotel has a gold roof cantilevered above the pavement from metal poles. The carpeted space underneath the roof is bathed in light, and the people under it look vivid and somehow frenetic. The women balancing on spiked heels, the men gesturing with lit phones. Rachel came here in early May, I know now. I imagine her ducking under the canopy, the gold light blazing on her dark head and bare shoulders.

I push open the revolving doors and cross a lobby with the restaurant and bar at its far end. I imagine Liam climbing down from his stool and opening his arms.

I stop, swaying on my feet.

···

During our argument, I worked out that on the night Liam cheated on me I was at a party in Fulham. Before the party Martha and I went for tapas, peppers in oil and grilled bread and olives. The party was on the roof of a mansion block. There were friends from St. Andrews and I wore a white crocheted dress and felt lucky and con-tented. On the walk to the party, I sent Liam a message, and he wrote a similar one back. Before my sister arrived, maybe, or while she was in the toilets. He said he missed me.

I wonder if they longed for each other afterward, and if separately or together they tried to plan a way it could happen again. Liam said neither of them remembered it. I hope that's true. If she didn't remember it then she couldn't have ever been thinking about it when we were together.

She made both of us foolish. We were better than this. We had other concerns. We had bigger fish to fry.

Prince Street ends at the river. I climb down the hill to the towpath and call Martha. "It was Rachel. He cheated on me with Rachel."

"Oh, no," she says, and her voice is gratifyingly horrified. I start to explain that his work trip was to Oxford, not Manchester, but she inter-rupts me. "My parents want to help. They know a defense barrister in Oxford."

"That's kind of them. If it comes to that—"

"You need advice now."

"Maybe." The story comes out in a rush, and I realize that since learning the news I have been aching to tell someone. I've been framing and reframing it in my mind, and recasting the events of the last six months based around it.

I start to tell Martha about meeting Liam at the covered market, but she stops me before I've finished and says, "Nora, don't talk to anyone about this. I wish you hadn't told me that."

"Why?"

"Because now if I'm ever sworn to oath, and someone asks if you were angry with Rachel I have to say yes." She sighs. "You would have split up anyway. Please try not to think too much of it. You have other problems now."

➤ 59 ◄

Lewis once told me he lives in Jericho, not far from here. He gives me the address, and a few minutes later I'm on the step of a brick terraced house and he is opening the door and saying, "Come in."

I follow him up the stairs to his flat. The living room is clean and lit by lamps. He has a green couch, bookshelves, and a low table holding a record player. From across the room, I can see the record turning, wobbling a little. A racing bicycle leans against one wall, under a poster from a heist film, three people running, their legs akimbo, in exaggerated vanishing point perspective. Lewis disappears into the kitchen and returns with two bottles of beer.

"Do you think I did it?"

"No."

My shoulders drop, and I can look at him properly now. He wears a red-checked flannel shirt. His expression is worried and intent.

"Moretti thinks I asked someone to assault her in Snaith."

"I know."

"I helped her look for him."

"The idea is that once she had been punished, you enjoyed the role. There are benefits to being close to a victim. It's like Munchausen by proxy."

"I didn't benefit from it. Am I officially a suspect?"

"Yes." He starts to peel the label from his beer. "She slept with your boyfriend."

"I don't see how that's my fault."

"That's not exactly the point."

"What else? What else do they find strange about me?"

"They think Rachel had been using the oven. A fireman noticed that the pot on one of the burners was still warm. It's unlikely an intruder would turn off a burner before leaving the scene, but you might, out of habit. Or so the house wouldn't burn down, since she left it to you."

"I can't remember," I say. "I don't think I went into the kitchen. What about the knife? What would I have done with the knife?"

"One theory," he says, "is that you didn't dispose of the knife at the scene. You tucked it into your waistband. At the police station, we know you went into the toilets alone. You wrapped the knife in paper, threw it in the bin, and that night it was loaded with the rest of the rubbish and brought to the landfill."

"That's absurd. Wouldn't Moretti have noticed?"

"It was a short blade." He puts his head back and rubs his face.

"Do you think I'm going to be charged?"

"No."

"Why?"

"We found a partial footprint. A men's Lonsdale, with blood on it."

The footprint doesn't eliminate me, he says, since I may have had an accomplice. My body turns leaden. The new information washes over me and I'm too tired to speak. Lewis notices and moves into the kitchen, leaving me to sink in privacy. Sometime later, he returns and hands me a bowl of ramen. We eat while listening to the record.

"Can you forgive her?" he asks.

"Yes," I say. "I think so."

When we finish our ramen, he rinses the bowls. It starts to rain, and I consider asking him if I can stay.

He lends me an umbrella. At the bottom of the stairs, as I lean on the point of the umbrella, he pulls me toward him and kisses me.

Only for a second, and then I am outside, my heart racing, the struts of the umbrella snapping open above me.

➤ 60 ⬅

I think I understand now why people don't leave when a war comes, why even residents with the means to leave stayed in a city like Sarajevo as danger drew closer. A mixture of disbelief and bargaining. If I stay, the war won't come.

I could drive to the airport and leave her car in short-stay parking. At an airline desk, I could buy a ticket to a country without an extradition treaty with England.

The police might have placed a travel alert on my passport, but that isn't what stops me. He stabbed Rachel eleven times. If I leave now, the police will consider it an admission of guilt, and he will never be caught.

⇒ 61 ⇐

I send myself up and down the aqueduct. At some point Keith will decide to go for a walk, or he will follow me. I carry pepper spray and the straight razor. The difficult part will be knowing when to stop him. He has to do enough damage for the police to take it seriously, but neither of us is going to die. The detectives must know that he is the violent one, not me, and not to trust anything he has told them.

Along the path, the brambles are shaped into hollow globes, and sparrows fly through them. I walk south toward Oyster Pond.

I have to forgive her or else sacrifice our last six months together. In a way, I don't entirely blame her. If she wanted to switch, to see what it was like to be the other of us, the one who stayed safely at the party that night, at dinner with my boyfriend. Or she just drank too much and stopped caring. Bitch, I think, and the venom does nothing to how much I miss her.

From part of the aqueduct, you can see the back of her house. The white wooden siding, the chimney, the two sheltering elms. Steam rises from the chimney, like someone is at home, but only because we left the boiler on so the pipes don't burst.

I wait for her to come outside. Or for Fenno to lunge into view at one of the windows. It hasn't gotten any easier to believe she's gone. At Oyster Pond, I test the pepper spray to make sure it isn't frozen. I do this on every other walk. If he doesn't come for me soon, it will be all used up.

⇒ 62 ⇐

Two constables are waiting for me in front of the Hunters. They've seen me before I notice them, they've been watching me come down the road. I know the area better than they do. I know places to hide around the aqueduct. The woods are the most dense by Oyster Pond, that's where I have to go, and I'm plotting this out, waiting for the right moment, but their eyes are fixed on me and I continue toward them. Full of rage, the length of the high street. They're wasting time. If they had waited a little longer, Keith would have come after me.

They step forward, reading me my rights while opening the door of the patrol car. They don't use handcuffs. During the drive to Abingdon, I focus on the landscape through the window to stop my throat from closing. They didn't give me time to change, and I still have pepper spray and the straight razor in my pocket.

The light box sign of the Thames Valley Police

appears. Much of it is the same as at other interviews. The room is identical, except one wall is a mirror, behind which other officers can watch us. I'm given a blue tracksuit to change into, and then left to wait in the interview room.

Moretti comes in and says, "Hello, Nora."

They were rehearsals, I realize now, all the interviews before this one. Moretti was practicing for this. He knows me now, and my weaknesses.

"We found some notes in your room. Is this your handwriting?"

"Yes."

He starts to read. " 'Harm compounding factors. Psychological damage to victim. Sustained attack on same victim. Use of weapon or weapon equivalent. Significant degree of premeditation.' " He leans back in his chair. "Why do you have the sentencing guidelines for grievous bodily harm?"

"Rachel thought the man who attacked her in Snaith might be caught for doing it again. I thought knowing the prison sentence for a similar crime would help me find him."

"Or," he says, "you wanted to know what your punishment might be."

"No."

"Where did you scatter her ashes?" he asks.

"Cornwall."

"Did anyone go with you?"

"No."

"None of Rachel's friends or family?"

"No."

"Why not? Did you ask them?"

"I wanted to be alone."

He smooths his suit jacket. "Did you ever bring anything onto the ridge? A picnic?"

"No."

"A witness saw you on the ridge carrying a plastic bag from Whistlestop."

"That's not possible."

"There is a Whistlestop in Paddington station. You told me you've made purchases from it. And that particular branch sells Tennent's Light Ale and Dunhills."

"Is the witness Keith? He made it up. Either they were his or you showed him photographs."

Moretti looks at the mirror, as though he wants to be sure someone has heard what I've just said. I wonder if I've already made a mistake. He remains silent for a moment. The witness must be Keith, or he would contradict me.

"You assembled the scene on the ridge," he says. "You wanted us to think Rachel had a stalker. Two days after her murder, you started to worry we might not find it, so you reported it yourself."

"No."

"Why were you on the ridge?"

"I wanted to see her house."

He leaves the room. For a long time I sit with my hands on my lap. They're watching me somewhere, on a video monitor, a small, still figure staring ahead. It must be meant to make me nervous, but it's a relief to be alone. They have thirty-six hours to charge me.

His boss, DCI Bristowe, will have to approve. He might be in her office now. I imagine she has been watching us, and I wish she would interview me herself. We've never spoken, she can't be convinced of my guilt. I imagine her in a suit, a coffee on her desk, rubbing her shoulders, wondering if she can go home. It will look bad for her, and her department, to charge two suspects that CPS declines to prosecute.

There isn't a clock in the interview room. Moretti wears a watch but its face is hidden under his sleeve. I don't know how much time passes. I look at the mirror to try to see shapes behind it. I listen for sounds in the building, and when I don't hear any I become frightened that we are the only ones in it.

"Is Lewis here?"

"No. DS Lewis has been suspended."

"Why?"

"Professional misconduct."

They don't let me sleep for very long. It seems like only a few minutes pass between when I enter the cell and when I am back in the room with Moretti. He drinks a tea and doesn't offer me one.

"Tell me about your relationship with Paul Wheeler."

I try to hide my surprise, but I'm sure Moretti caught it, a twitch. "We met for the first time a few weeks ago. I think he attacked Rachel in Snaith."

"He sent you roses."

"He was harassing me. He sent the flowers to scare me."

"Have you given Paul Wheeler any gifts? Have you lent or given him money?"

"No."

"What are the terms of your agreement?"

"We don't have an agreement."

Moretti stands and stretches. There are wrinkles on the back of his suit jacket. "Nothing you did with Lewis was illegal," he says, "but a jury will want to know why you slept with a case detective so soon after the murder."

Later, he pulls a sheet of paper toward him and lowers his head to read. " 'I'm unhappy. I don't feel like myself. I'm scared this won't go away.' " He continues, and I lean forward, my hands twisting on my lap. He's reading my psychologist's notes. I thought they were sealed.

Moretti finishes reading and we sit with the paper on the table between us. "When you found out that Rachel caused so much unhappiness, you must have been very angry with her."

"I didn't know about Liam until you told me."

He looks again at the mirror. Moretti still hasn't mentioned the weapon. If the murderer used a knife from her house, my fingerprints might be on it. I've cooked using those knives.

➤ 63 ◄

A duty solicitor comes to see me. She introduces herself as Amrita Ghosh. "Have I been charged?" I ask.

"No," she says. "I'm here to explain what might happen next."

Her voice is candid and direct, and she meets my eyes. I can't tell if she thinks I'm guilty. I suppose she might not have an opinion. She is here to share general information, not offer me advice. She might not have reviewed the case in any detail.

She starts with what I already know. After my arrest, the police have thirty-six hours before they must either charge or release me. If I am released, the police will likely continue to consider me as a suspect and to build the case against me, unless new evidence eliminates me.

The solicitor doesn't do anything to confuse me. She never asks how I am coping. She makes it clear that she is a neutral party. If I am charged, I will remain in custody while an Oxfordshire prosecutor decides if the evidence against me is strong enough to move to trial. If it is, I will appear before a magistrate to enter a plea. If I plead guilty, negotiations will begin between my defense counsel and the prosecutor. If I plead not guilty, the magistrate will either set bail or remand me into custody until the trial.

"It is my duty to tell you that there is a sentence reduction for a guilty plea. The prosecutor might also adjust the charge from murder to man-slaughter. It depends on the details of the offense."

"What's the average length of time in prison after a guilty manslaughter plea?"

"Three years."

"What's the average if you plead not guilty to murder and are convicted?"

"Twenty years."

She holds my eyes. I don't think she believes I'm innocent.

The difference between being released at thirty-three or forty-nine.

I won't do well in cross-examination. At York Crown Court some defendants remained composed and patient. Others became emotional, to the jury's distaste. The juries appeared to prefer when defendants kept calm, and I won't be able to.

The visit from the duty solicitor was not about due process, it was the first application of pressure. They could have waited until I was charged, but they want to be sure I have time before the magistrate's hearing to consider it. Three or twenty years.

➤ 64 ⬅

"Are you tired?" he asks.

"Yes."

He smiles at me. For a moment I think he will let me go. The silence stretches between us.

"Your fingerprints are on the banister post."

I watch his expression closely. "Which one?"

"The one you tied the dog's lead around."

"I must have touched it on a different visit."

"They're close to the ground. To reach there, you would have had to kneel on the floor." He straightens his tie. "One of the prints is in the dog's blood."

"Show me a photograph of it."

He leaves the room. My breathing turns loud and ragged. I can't remember if detectives are allowed to lie during an interview. It's such a huge point of law, I can't believe I don't know it. He might be allowed to say anything.

The minutes stretch on. I try to stare through the black mirror, and my reflection is appalled and ashen. He wants to retire. How important is it to him to leave after a success? I never considered it before.

I didn't touch the banister post that day, but I did touch the dog. I put my hand against his side while he was hanging. I knew he was dead, but I still wanted to comfort him.

I must have left fingerprints somewhere else in the house. All he would have to do is change the label on where the print was found. The house has been industrially cleaned now. I won't be able to prove him wrong.

➤ 65 ◄

Moretti doesn't return, and a constable leads me to the cell.

He's fitting me up. When I asked about the defensive injuries, he shrugged. He might decide to remember a scratch or a bruise on me.

I don't sleep. Instead I pretend to be a juror, listening to the evidence and the witnesses. I don't know if it will be clear that the police are crooked, or if something about me will make it easy for them to believe.

A constable unlocks the door and says, "Follow me, please."

Sunlight falls over us as we walk down the corridor. It must be Thursday morning. I can't tell from her face if in a few minutes she will charge or release me.

An officer hands me my clothes and bag. Moretti isn't in the room. I wonder if he's watching on a monitor somewhere else in the building. I'm not being charged. He must have lied about the prints on the banister.

I hurry away from the police station. The morning is cool and damp, the sun behind a scrim of gray cloud. Giddiness bursts up my legs and into my chest. I dig my nails into the sides of my arms, sailing down the road.

By the time I reach Marlow, the Emerald Gate has opened. I order scallion pancakes, chow fun, and dumplings. I eat greedily, tearing the pancakes with my hands, scooping mouthfuls of food. While I eat, I don't think of anything but how it tastes.

After the bowls are scraped clean, I lean back in my chair and look out the window and wonder what I am supposed to do next.

At the station last night I started to make plans. I didn't mean to, but couldn't help it. Plans to travel. To sleep rough.

⇥ 66 ⇤

I return to the Hunters to pack my things. Tonight I will stay with Martha in London, and the thought makes me heavy with relief.

Before I stow my laptop, I open it on the bed.

The screen brightens. I haven't checked his name in over a week, since before Cornwall.

Paul Wheeler violated his parole. Over the weekend he assaulted a woman in Holbeck, South Leeds. Milly Athill. The name sounds familiar, but I can't place it. He followed her into her home. The charge against him will be much more severe this time. He committed the crime while he was on probation, and it's a repeat offense. It was a sustained attack on one victim. The prosecutor will likely be able to prove psychological damage to the victim.

Her brother was upstairs, by chance, and he and Milly were able to overpower Paul.

The maximum sentence for grievous bodily harm is life imprisonment, and the solicitor interviewed for the article expects him to receive that or close to it.

Is that enough? I ask Rachel. Is it over?

I speak to Lewis. Moretti had a trace on my car, apparently, the day I went to his house. He's in Brighton now, and he tells me about his flat. You can see the channel from every room, he says, even the bathroom. He says that after a constable told him I'd been released, he ate chips and vinegar on the beach to celebrate. He asks if I want to come visit and I say yes, soon.

I look down at the article again. "Would anyone

know you've been suspended yet? If, for example, you called a prison and asked to speak to an inmate."

I walk through Marlow while waiting for his call. Down Meeting House Lane, down Redgate. Past the church, past the firehouse, past the tennis court. I'm on the common, facing the village hall, when Lewis calls.

"I spoke to Paul Wheeler," he says, and his voice is careful and measured. "He says Rachel was his girlfriend."

My eyes skitter away, and it looks like the clock is falling out of the village hall.

"It sounds like they only went out a few times, when she was a teenager. He said he hated his name, he always told girls he was called Clive. She wouldn't have been able to find him. He didn't admit to the assault, but he said they had an argument, and soon after he moved to Newcastle for work."

"Is he making it up?"

"He said he gave her a mask. Does that sound familiar?"

The white carnival mask, with a curved beak. She hung it on the wall in her room.

"She probably thought the police would consider the crime more seriously if it were a stranger."

"But why wouldn't she tell me?"

"It happens," he says. "Victims often don't tell their families when they knew the person who beat or raped them."

After the call ends, I sit on a bench under the yews and turn my face up to the thrashing branches. The wind roars, growing louder and louder.

I remember what happened at the Cross Keys now. The red half-height doors of the toilets. I didn't go in with a man, I went in with Rachel. I had barely seen her all night. And she said, "I've been talking to someone. I think I've met someone."

I know what Lewis meant. If she told me she knew him, she wouldn't be able to forgive me if, for even a second, I suggested it was somehow her fault.

But I don't understand why she thought I would have.

After some time, I leave the common and return to my room to finish packing. Milly Athill. Before closing the laptop, I search through the other articles about Paul Wheeler and finally find the name in one of the first reports after the crime that sent him to prison. Before the assault, the victim was at a pub with her best friend, Milly.

Her brother was upstairs at the time. He's a rugby player who lives in Dublin, but he happened to be at her house. What a coincidence.

I always wondered why the police don't use bait more often. Apparently so did they.

"Are you checking out?" the manager asks hopefully.

"Yes."

She charges me for the night I spent in jail.

⇀ 67 ↽

"I thought you would move," I say. Louise, on her own in front of the service station, looks at me as though I'm mad.

"No," she says. "No, I haven't moved."

She could be in Camden. The gas ring. The tratt. Louise frowns. I should say something else, but I can't, and I start to fill the car with petrol for the drive to London.

Her decision to stay seems pathological. Louise watches me and parts her mouth just enough to let out a flat stream of smoke. A familiarity opens between us, because of our resemblance, maybe, and I think she knows what I meant, and that it would be all right for me to tell her who I am. I am about to start but find I can't. The only way I can think to begin is—my sister was murdered. My sister was murdered.

"Do you want one?" asks Louise. She wears the same outfit as always, a navy shirt, black skirt, and apron, but with a duffle coat wrapped over it. On the ledge beside her are a pack of cigarettes and a glass of mint tea steaming into the cold air.

I replace the pump and join her. As she offers me the pack, I notice the dark red marks on her hand, from when she was burned with a cigarette or stabbed with a screwdriver.

"Yes," I say, "cheers." I bend toward the lighter, straighten, exhale. I move around her so I am also leaning against the restaurant window. There is a jet in the distance, and it sounds like a wall breaking apart.

Louise stares at a van parked on the grass on the far side of the Bristol Road.

"Why would I move?" she asks.

"I'm sorry," I say. "It's none of my business." She shifts toward me, rolling onto her shoulder against the glass, and waits. "It must be difficult for you to go past that every day."

"Past what?"

"Where Callum died."

"He didn't die in the accident," she says. "He woke up after the surgery. He died the next night."

"From what?"

"Complications."

The sensation is like missing a stair. Of course, I think, before the thought has even formed into words.

"There was a collision here," said Rachel. She

pointed out the window. "A man and a woman."

"Did they survive?"

"One did."

"Which one?"

"The woman."

Sunlight warms the top of my head, then vanishes, like a hand pressing down and lifting. Why? I should have asked. Why did only one survive?

Callum must have been the subject of the coroner's inquest in October. Rachel never told me the death was under review. After the inquest, she invented a reason for driving past the accident site. She wanted to show it to me. I wonder if she was disappointed that I didn't suspect anything, or if it was a relief.

"None of her injuries came from the crash," she said. "It's a good thing he didn't make it. He would have killed her."

I turn to Louise, but it feels like a counter-motion, and something else is rotating beneath me. She gathers her cigarettes and lighter, her glass, and nods at me before going inside. Through the window, I watch her hang up her duffle coat and tie the strings on her apron. Waves of heat sweep over me. Rachel wanted revenge, and she must have grown tired of waiting to find the man who attacked her. Louise moves in and out of the glare, and I watch her while I call Joanna.

"Was Rachel at the coroner's inquest in October?" I ask.

"No," she says.

A line of rippling birds flies low over the trees.

"Was she one of his nurses?"

"Yes."

I close my eyes and wrap my hand over my forehead.

"I don't remember all the particulars," says Joanna. "Can I call you back when I have it in front of me?"

"Have what in front of you?"

"The transcript from the inquest."

"Is that a public document?"

"Yes."

"I'm on my way to the hospital now, will you make a copy for me?"

"All right. I'm going to be in rounds, but I'll leave it at the nurses' station for you."

"Can you tell me anything you remember?"

"It was a good result. The cause of death wasn't negligence."

The sounds around me sharpen and separate. "Who was the patient?"

"Callum Hold."

"How did he die?"

"The latch on his intravenous drip broke. He overdosed."

"Does he have any family?"

"Yes, he had a brother."

"What was his name?"

"Martin Hold."

The inquest transcript begins with a précis from the coroner. The patient was brought to the John Radcliffe after a road accident on 22 September. The consultant surgeon recommended reconstructive work to repair internal bleeding. The surgery was successful. On the morning following the surgery, the patient was awake and in stable condition. Shortly after six that night he was pronounced dead.

The cause of death was not complications from surgery, as originally suspected. He died from an overdose of fentanyl, a medical heroin. The drip was meant to give him a painkiller at regular intervals. When its latch broke, the fluid flooded his veins.

An expert witness testified on faulty medical equipment. He believed the hospital staff did nothing wrong. Despite all precautions, equipment sometimes fails. Faulty equipment is the cause of one-fourth of all deaths in hospital.

Never, never, never, never. Kill, kill, kill, kill, kill.

Martin Hold. She told me his first name so I would remember it. So I would recognize it if anything happened to her.

If nothing did happen, if she made it to St. Ives, I doubt she would have ever confessed. But maybe it would have weighed on her too much, and one day she would have called me and said, "I've got something to tell you."

I find the important part halfway through the transcript, hunched on the bench across from Casualty. Martin visited his brother in hospital. He was alert at the time, and they had a long conversation.

I cover my face with my hands. Rachel must have asked Callum about Louise's injuries, or threatened him, and he told his brother.

In A&E Louise is wheeled past Rachel and into a room. Rachel starts to examine her. She presents like someone who has been in a road accident, but the strange thing is some of her wounds appear to have started to heal, and some of them already have bandages.

Rachel limps in and out of pubs and betting shops in Hull. Where would a violent man go, where would a monster go.

She had a way, sometimes. When she wanted to. I can hear her voice, burry and low, and she says, "When I was seventeen a man beat me up." She waits. She says, "Do you want to tell me what happened to you?"

∙ ∙ ∙

Even if the detectives read the inquest transcript, Martin doesn't stand out. He doesn't accuse her and he doesn't sound aggrieved. Or he does, but not with her. He says there should be consequences for the manufacturer, so other families don't go through what he has gone through. The coroner advises him to seek the advice of a solicitor for damages.

The transcript is a public document, like a trial record, but surely some of it would have been redacted if the coroner's office were giving it to a member of the public instead of back to the hospital. Like Callum's medical records, and all the contact information for his next of kin.

"I need your help," I say. The service station café is empty and Louise looks at me, with a dishcloth in one hand. "My name's Nora Lawrence."

"I know who you are," she says. This whole time, I thought I was the one watching her.

"Did you tell Rachel how you got your injuries?"

"Yes."

She regards me with her small, calm face.

"Rachel broke the latch on his drip."

Louise closes her eyes. "I know," she says.

First we drive to Cirencester and Martha's family's estate. A long gravel drive, a row of poplars. Louise waits in the car. Martha's mum answers the door, and when she sees me her hand covers her mouth.

"Hello, Lily. Is Martha here?"

"No, darling, she isn't."

"Oh, I must be supposed to meet her in town. Do you mind if I use the loo before I go?"

Her mum goes into the kitchen, to call Martha, I imagine. I slip into the hall. The cabinet is downstairs, and unlocked. I remember that Martha shrugged. No small children in the house.

I call good-bye to Lily on my way out. On the doorstep, she grasps both my shoulders and kisses me. I return to the car and settle my bag between my seat and the door. Louise looks at it, but doesn't ask.

Sixty Rutland Street, Stoke-on-Trent.

I call the second of the two telephone numbers and ask for Martin.

"No, he's not here," says a young man. "He isn't here until four."

"Thanks. Can you remind me of your address?"

"Five thirty Waterloo."

It is a paint shop, also in Stoke, around the corner from his home.

We drive north on the M5. Louise tests the recorder on her phone, and we listen to our voices from a few moments ago. Her voice sounds high and youthful, and mine sounds clear and taut. "So it works, then," she says.

Past Bishop's Cleeve. Past Redditch. It's unfamiliar countryside. I think that's a good thing. I think the strangeness of this might paralyze me if I were on a familiar route.

The road to Stoke is broad and nearly empty, but I drive like I am traveling across central London in the rain. I study each road sign as though I've just missed an exit, and my heart pounds when a driver merges well ahead of me.

"He said if I left he was going to kill me," says Louise. "I didn't ask Rachel to do it, but I told her about him."

They grew up in Stoke, I learned from Callum's obituary. They had a sister, Kirsty, but the obituary didn't say what happened to her. Were they bad then? Can you learn to do what they did to Rachel and Louise? If their dad beat them I wish he had finished the job.

Past Birmingham. Past Stafford. The nervousness fades and is replaced with a low and solid dread. Neither of us speaks.

Louise will talk to him first and record the conversation. The recording won't be admissible in court, but her account of what he tells her will be. And the police can listen to it, and the jury can be made aware that a tape exists. We park on Waterloo Road a block from the paint shop.

"Are you sure?" I ask her again.

"He likes me," she says. "We never talked about what Callum did. He has no reason to be suspicious."

"You didn't go to the funeral," I say, remembering.

"My best friend went. She told Martin I was still too distraught to leave the house." I shake my head and she says, "I know. Quite clever," and climbs out of the car.

I put my hood up. Martin lives in a terrace of brick houses. Most of the houses in the terrace are empty. Some have estate agent signs and others do not. The terrace backs onto an alley, and I walk up it, past the low sheds and garages. Strange Victorian buttresses separate each property. One of the bins has been tipped over, and as I step around the stream of rubbish, I hope it is his, I hope the kids here hate him. I count the lots until number sixty. It doesn't look any different from the others. Stained brick, buttresses, shed.

Not far from here is a corner shop. I could buy kitchen roll, a jug of fuel, and matches. This is so clear I may have already done it. I imagine the weight of the jug rocking in my hand as the fuel glugs out. It splashes on my feet. It darkens the brick. I imagine the smell of petrol. I imagine carefully wiping the fuel from my hands before lighting the kitchen roll.

I consider the house. I consider the house burning, but I would only be doing him a favor, destroying evidence.

I keep thinking of the officers swarming the woods behind her house. They had seemed so certain of the direction, that they'd find something. Then and all the nights since, like a clock steadily ticking, he has been here.

Louise meets me in the alley behind his house. "It was him," she says. Her teeth chatter. "He told me he took care of it."

She dials the police station in Abingdon, which we decided would act on the information more quickly than the one in Stoke. "My name's Louise Rosten. A friend of mine just confessed to the murder of Rachel Lawrence."

The desk officer transfers her to a detective whose voice I don't recognize. Louise tells him about the confession and says she's scared he's going to hurt her now. She describes what he did to the dog. It still hasn't come out in the press, only the police and the emergency workers who came to her house that day could know about it, and the person who did it. The detective asks her to hold the line. Her teeth don't stop chattering.

When he returns, the detective says he has spoken to the station in Stoke, which will send patrol cars to the shop to arrest him. In the meantime, he asks Louise to wait somewhere safe.

• • •

I went cliff jumping once in Dorset, so I recognize this, that I am paralyzed with fear. Even with the handful of other shops, the block is quieter than I expected. The shop walls are made of plaster that was scraped into crescents before it dried. There is no side or rear exit. The building stands near the middle of the block. The lights are on, weakly, and I think I can see the shape of a person through the window display.

Louise will be gone by now. We agreed she would take a train back to Oxford. The detective will call her in for a full statement.

The police will be here soon. The Stoke police station is two miles away, but there might be a patrol car closer by. I command myself to move, which is as useless as when I told myself to jump off a fifty-foot cliff into Mirror Lake, which I did eventually, out of some combination of weariness and fatalism, like I had already done it and died, and I move toward the door. I take my hood down.

Martin Hold is behind the counter, and at first his face is blank and open. Then something slides over it. He recognizes me. It is as obvious as the moment when the friend you are meeting first sees you.

He is younger than I expected. Not far past thirty. He wears a gray sweater with holes at the hem. He has red in his hair. There is a deep wrinkle across his forehead. He has a short beard, and his hair is grown out. He looks like anyone, but just underneath it is the adolescent, when his skin was worse and his hairline shaved back. He is so familiar, like one of the boys we grew up with.

I don't remember starting to cry but my face is wet.

"Hello," I say, in the voice I used to have. I can tell that my face is contorting.

He stares at me without saying anything. I lift the pistol from my bag and point it at him.

"Roll your sleeves up."

His eyes are wide. He lowers his head and slowly pushes up one sleeve.

Both of his arms are covered in red marks. One of the scars forms a neat half circle around his forearm. The dog's jaw. My body is shuddering now. I want him dead. It's what Rachel would want me to do, I know that now.

"Did it take a long time?" I ask.

He continues to watch me, and I don't think he will answer.

"No," he says.

I lower the gun and walk outside. The road is quiet under a gray sky. I can hear the sirens. At first I think I am imagining them, a disruption somewhere in the distance, but the sound grows steadily louder, and I start to move away from it.

Both of us went cliff jumping in Dorset. The water was so clear that after Rachel jumped I could see her on the other side, plunging down through the center of what looked like a cascading, clear swell.

⤜ 68 ⤛

Martha is waiting for me at a pub in Battersea. It's warm enough now that people sit outside cafés on the King's Road.

I turn down an alley. A man appears at the far end, walking toward me, and I consider turning back. As we pass, he nods at me, and then I am out the other side, and rushing across the bright road.

I know I'm going to be all right. And I know I will never stop missing her.

What's your favorite thing about Cornwall? I asked her. But it wasn't what I meant. I meant, what's your favorite thing about being alive?

And she said, Well.

She said, To start—

→ Acknowledgments ←

I wish to thank: Michael Adams, my first reader; Emily Forland, my agent; and Lindsey Schwoeri, my editor.

The three of you are ferociously intelligent, wry, and kind. You have each made this thrilling in different ways, and I am enormously grateful.

All at the Michener Center for Writers and Yaddo.

Everyone at Penguin.

My friends, and especially Nick Cherneff, Kate DeOssie, Donna Erlich, Jackie Friedman, Allison Kantor, Suchi Mathur, Justine McGowan, Madelyn Morris, Althea Webber, and Marisa Woocher.

My aunts, Kassia Dellabough, Marlitt Dellabough, and Liana Rödegård, who have been the best possible source for research.

All of my family, and especially my parents, Jon Berry and Robin Dellabough.

And Jeff Bruemmer.

⇢ About the Author ⇠

Flynn Berry is a graduate of the Michener Center for Writers, and has been awarded a Yaddo residency. This is her first novel.

Center Point Large Print
600 Brooks Road / PO Box 1
Thorndike, ME 04986-0001 USA

(207) 568-3717

US & Canada:
1 800 929-9108
www.centerpointlargeprint.com